The Library Room

Varnie Cumbest

PublishAmerica
Baltimore

First printing

PublishAmerica has allowed this work to remain exactly as the author intended, verbatim, without editorial input.

Hardcover 978-1-4489-5518-3
Softcover 978-1-4512-0471-1
Pocketbook 978-1-4512-8366-2
PUBLISHED BY PUBLISHAMERICA, LLLP
www.publishamerica.com
Baltimore

Printed in the United States of America

I would like to dedicate this book:

To my daughter Jackie Pappas, who encouraged me to write and follow my dream. Without her constant support I would have never finished the book.

To my granddaughters Chrystal Zinni and Aliki Pappas who inspired me to keep trying and not give up.

I want to thank Melissa A. Balcombe for her work in editing this book. Her patience and willingness to help is greatly appreciated.

CHAPTER 1

Katie remained at the kitchen table longer than usual this morning: long after breakfast was over, the kids had left for school, and Papa had gone back to his room. She sat there, thinking of what he had said about her old percolator coffeepot and how it had died. A natural death he called it. It simply overheated and burned out! But she suspected the real reason was that it was overworked. She used it too much. She made at least two pots of coffee in it every day. She would brew one in the morning, one in the afternoon, and sometimes a third pot on weekends when company came. The pot held up to twelve cups, but she never made more than six at any one time. She quickly did the math in her head: twice six equals twelve, minus the two cups that Papa drank. She estimated she left one cup in each pot which left her drinking the rest, and that worried her. She was drinking up to eight cups a day, and that was just too much, and she knew it.

Papa and the kids didn't care for coffee all that much even though Papa drank two cups in the mornings. He liked to stay at the table after breakfast. After the kids left for school, he would sip on his second cup, talking with her while she cleaned the dishes and straightened up the kitchen. He called it their staff meetings. It was the only time he would talk to her about himself, and she used it to question him about his health and well being. She would ask him a series of questions. Did he have any aches or pains? Did he walk yesterday? Did he sleep well the night before? Was he feeling good today? He would look up at her, flex his bicep muscles in his arm, and tell her not worry. He was still a young man, and he had all the normal aches and pains to prove it.

He never would drink any coffee with her in the afternoons though, and she always wondered why until one day, he told her. Katie had just made a fresh pot one afternoon, and asked Papa to come in the kitchen and have a cup with her. He told her then, the one side effect he suffered from drinking coffee was that if he drank that cup with her now he would lose a lot of sleep and that he would be up all through the night going to the bathroom. She never asked him to drink coffee in the afternoons with her again.

The kids very seldom drank any of it at all, and when they did, it was always in the mornings with her and Papa, and only because she kept asking them to. She knew they never cared for it, and she was glad they didn't because everyone was always telling her too much caffeine was not good for the human body, and coffee had a lot of caffeine in it. A neighbor just told her yesterday, that leg cramps were caused from the caffeine found in coffee. She didn't really believe that, but she did read in a magazine the night before that drinking coffee anytime other than in the mornings, was not the right thing to do. Two of the side effects the magazine listed were that it would make one hyper, and cause one to stay awake at night. Papa even told her that drinking too much of it would keep her bladder full, and make her go the bathroom more often, and even cause her to start mumbling and talking to herself. She definitely didn't believe in the mumbling part either.

She had to admit, she was beginning to talk to herself a lot, and it did seem like she had been making more trips to the bathroom these past days. It worried her more that she was allowing something like drinking coffee in the afternoons to become a habit with her. She sat there for a few minutes longer, weighing the pros and cons of her new habit, and wondering if her feeling tired most of the time had anything to do with her new addiction. Then she got up and walked down the stairs to the basement to finish the washing she started the night before.

"I'm hooked on it," she mumbled to herself as she entered the basement. "I don't like the control it has over me, but what can I do? I love the stuff!"

She emptied the clothes from the washer, and put them in the dryer, set the timer, and walked back up the few steps that led to the kitchen, and other areas of the house. From there, she could listen for the timer while she finished the rest of her housework. She walked to the window and opened the blinds to let some light into the house. It was starting to cloud up outside. She noticed it had rained a little yesterday, and it would probably rain again today, but she wasn't going to complain. She was just glad it hadn't started to rain yet. She convinced herself that if it had rained, that she might not have rushed out of the house this morning, gone to town, and got her new electric percolator coffeepot. She really would have complained this afternoon when her work was done and there was no coffee to drink!

She left the window and walked into the living room to begin her housework.

"I don't know why I'm so sleepy," she told herself, putting her hand over her mouth and yawning. "I slept good last night. I guess it's this dreary weather we're having. I'm getting a late start I know, but there's not really that much to do," she said as she pulled the vacuum cleaner from the closet and looked around the room. "If I can just stay awake, and get started now, I can finish up here, and have some time left over to think about that book I've wanted to write."

Ever since her high school days when she was writing poems for her class mates, Katie wanted to write a novel. Now years later, ideas popped up in her head, and she always tried to find the time to write some of them down, but she just couldn't. Taking care of a seventy-year-old man who thought he was forty, a son who thought he should be put in charge of his sister, and a daughter that fantasized she was in every movie she saw, left her with no time. It was a full time job for her, and finding time to sit down, think about ideas, then write them down on paper was a luxury that she just didn't have.

She finished vacuuming the floors and started dusting off the furniture. Then she stopped, walked back into the kitchen, and got out her brand new percolator coffee pot. She rinsed it out at the sink, and put the old one in the box the new one came in and left them both on the bar. She dried her hands with a paper towel, then walked back, and sat down at the table. She kicked her legs out and let the past events of the morning run across her mind. She recalled Papa telling her just last week that while he was sitting at the breakfast table, sipping on his first cup that he believed the old coffeepot is on its last leg. Sure enough, this morning seven days later, while they both were still drinking their first after-breakfast cup, they watched as the heating element in the pot burned out. That ended the life of the old coffeepot.

She continued sitting there, leaning back in the chair, hardly batting an eye. She was picturing in her mind the new box housing the old pot with its scoured bottom and the burned out cord hanging from it. The heat she remembered had been so intense when the old pot burned, that the area where the cord connected melted, preventing it from being removed. She remembered thinking how glad she was the kids had already left the table and didn't see the fire, or hear the explosion. They would not have been in a life-threatening situation, nor would they have gotten hurt but still she thought that they probably would have had nightmares if they had witnessed it.

She closed her eyes and shook her head as if trying to shake off her own nightmares. It was a chilling situation she had to admit. One she hoped would never happen again. The fire, the smell, and then the messy foam she sprayed on it. She tried to bolt it all from her mind but it kept coming back. It wasn't really a fire, more like a smothered flame, she remembered. There as a flash, sparks flew up from around the bottom of the pot, or maybe it was from the cord. She didn't remember which. One spark hit her on the finger, another landed on the table, burning a small brown hole in the white table cloth. As she jumped up from the table in her haste to pull the cord from the wall, she knocked over a chair, almost spilling the rest of the coffee all over herself. It all happened so fast and ended so quickly, it really upset her.

She and Papa both stayed at the table another ten minutes, just talking about it. It was indeed a miracle that the pot wasn't knocked over, spilling the rest of the coffee all over her, and all over Papa too. They could have both been burned or at best had their clothes ruined from the coffee stains left on them. Smiling to herself, Katie sat up straight in the chair, closed her eyes, and pictured the brown stains all over Papa's trousers. She felt ashamed and thought of how patient he had been over the past years. Never once did he complain as he put up with the many reasons she had given him for keeping that old coffeepot.

"I was afraid something like that was about to happen," she remembered saying to him, after she recovered from the shock and embarrassment of knocking over the chair. "I knew that sooner or later, I'd have to buy a new one. I guess I just hoped it would be later. It has been a good one though," she said, sitting back down, and reaching her hand out across the table to show him the small blister that had began to rise on her finger. "I hope I can find another one just like it!"

She remembered standing the chair back up and walking to the sink. Then forgetting what she went there for, she turned around went back and sat down at the table. She noticed the almost sick look on Papa's face as he sat there, frozen like a statue and not making a sound, just staring at his almost empty cup. For a moment she thought he had either been hit by a flying spark, or was just sadden over the loss of the old pot. She was about to ask him if he was alright when he suddenly stood up, looked straight at her, and without saying a word, told her she was responsible, and it was all her fault.

"No," he said, as he sat back down just as sudden as he had gotten up. The expression on his face told her, he was just saddened over the loss of the old coffeepot.

"That pot didn't just quit, it got old and died. Even that pot couldn't last forever, made a many good cups of hot coffee though. You better put some cold water on that blister. It's going to start hurting soon if you don't. I hope you can find another one too but I'm afraid your days of making coffee in a percolator coffeepot are over."

She looked up at him, surprised that he would say such a thing "Why?" she asked, feeling a little shocked, and realizing he was right. She was responsible and yet relieved that he wasn't hit by a flying spark. At the same time she was anxious to know why he thought her days of making coffee in a percolator coffeepot were coming to an end.

"What do you mean?" she asked.

"I like making coffee in a percolator pot. Not just for the coffee it makes either, but the sound of it perking. It relaxes me, making my work seem a lot easier. I don't know what I'd do, if I couldn't make coffee in it ever morning. I don't like those new coffee makers you see on the market today. They are pretty and cute I'll admit. They make coffee a lot quicker, and their probably more convenient to use. I think that's why a lot of people buy them but they don't keep the coffee hot! For someone like me, who likes their second and third cup hot when they get it, I wouldn't recommend buying one! Their just not worth the trouble it takes, to keep heating up the refills! I bought one a few years back. Remember?" she continued. "Used it for one whole month, after that I stopped and gave it to a neighbor. The first cup, I remember was real hot, after that, the rest were just luke warm. Luke warm!" She liked that phrase. She didn't know why or where the connection was, but somehow it seemed to go good with warm coffee.

"We had to heat each of the remaining cups up in the microwave," she continued, "before we could drink them."

"You remember that, don't you? You always complained about your second cup being cold and not as good. Something about heating them up in the microwave changed their taste.

You would say, "You reckon you'd have to learn to drink them that way though."

"Yep", Papa said looking up from the table. "I remember, and I'm glad you bought that new pot when you did. If you hadn't, I think it would have been much easier for me to just stop drinking coffee. But you got to admit, we have been using that pot for a long time. Its more than served its purpose! We should have replaced it long ago when we could have got another one just like it. We both knew it was just a matter of time, before it stopped making coffee altogether, and now that it has. I just knew you'd rush out, like so many others have, and buy one of those new coffee makers. I figured you'd have to. That is if you still wanted to make coffee, because you wouldn't be able to find another percolator coffeepot. They are almost extinct you know. All you see in the stores now days are those new eye-catching, push-a-button-and-they-are-on-type coffee makers. They're just not making percolator coffeepots anymore!"

She remembered looking around and seeing a glass of cold water her daughter had left on the table. She poured it into a small bowl and put her finger in it. "Aah," she said aloud, after leaving it in the cold water for a few seconds then taking it out. She rubbed the small blister on her finger. "Cold water does stop the pain from hurting!"

Papa made several more remarks about the old coffeepot, how good it had been, and how he hoped she could find another one just like it. Then he picked up his cup, swallowed the last drop of coffee in it, and set it down on the table. For the first time since he started staying over after breakfast and drinking coffee with her, he left the kitchen without having his second cup of coffee.

CHAPTER 2

Katie sat there for a while longer after Papa had left, collecting her thoughts. Then she got up, walked to the bar, wrapped her hands around her new coffeepot, and felt the coolness of the cold water inside. Then she empted it, and filled it with newer cold water. She boiled it, empted it again, and refilled it with fresh cold water. She measured out the right amount of coffee, put the lid back on, and returned to dusting off the furniture. She wasn't ready just yet, to make a pot of coffee. It was too early.

But this afternoon, when she would be ready, she wanted to be sure everything else was right, so all she would have to do was plug the electric cord into the wall socket, and within five minutes, a pot of fresh percolated coffee would be made. She purposely left the cord unplugged.

This way, she told herself, she could have a fresh cup of coffee waiting for her just before she finished cleaning and straightening up the house.

She had just finished making up her own bed, when she heard the timer from the dryer go off.

"Good," she said to herself, "Just clean my daughter's room now, and I'm all finished!"

She walked back to the kitchen, plugged the cord into the wall socket, and waited to hear the sound of the coffee perking. She walked back down the stairs to the basement. Katie removed the clothes from the dryer, put them in a basket, and carried them up to her daughter's room.

She sat down on the one-sided rail daybed that her daughter insisted on having in her room. She folded her clothes and put them away. She picked up some papers and books off the floor, tidied up the desk, and made up her daughter's bed. She then walked over to the window, pulled the blind up to let some light in, and looked around the room.

There were numerous pictures and posters of different rock stars and classmates posing in weird and uncanny positions; they were spread about in no certain order all over the walls. And for a moment, as she continued staring at the pictures, she wondered if she would have decorated her own walls in such a manner when she was a teenager. She thought about that for another moment. Then decided if she did have a room to decorate as a teenager, she most certainly would not have displayed the pictures of her heroes in such a strange and bizarre manner. She turned and walked away from the window.

A sudden gust of bright sunlight burst into the room where she had opened the blinds; it hurt her eyes and made her feel tired and sleepy. For a moment, she thought about going back to her own room and lying down, but decided not to since this was the first time she'd been in her daughter's room in some time. She wanted to stay alert, look around, and find out for herself: why this past week, four teenage girls, friends from her daughter's school had visited everyday for the past four days. All five of them spent their entire time together, shut up in her daughter's bedroom with the door locked. It was then she also realized that they each brought backpacks with them, and since school was out, she was pretty sure those backpacks weren't filled with books. She didn't want to spy on them, and she didn't want to meddle in her daughter's business, but mothers did have a right to know what their children were up to.

There was a lot going through Katie's mind. She watched those girls bring a stepladder into the room, carry their heavy backpacks in each day, and they locked the door behind them. They would refuse to come out, even for a short break. It became pretty clear to her, that those girls and her daughter were up to something!

She rubbed her hand across her face, then tilted her head straight back, and looked up at the ceiling, mostly to rest her eyes, and almost passed out in shock.

"What in the world?" she heard herself saying as she stumbled back to the desk, and almost fell into the chair. Then she remembered the girls from the school, and the backpacks, and the locked door. She sat there at her daughter's desk, with her mouth wide open, staring straight up at the ceiling. She knew for the first time in four days, what those girls and he daughter had been up to. If she hadn't been cleaning her bedroom this morning, and seen it with her own eyes, she never would have believed it.

There it was, glowing in life-like color, right over her head, covering almost half of the ceiling wall. A full size basketball court! It was brilliantly drawn on the white ceiling wall by one of the girls. The replica was complete with screaming fans, two goals, a referee, and a brightly lit scoreboard showing the home team winning the basketball game.

There was more. At one end of the couch, presumably the home end, right beneath the goal and drawn on the highly-glossed wooden floor, was a large circle about the size of two round dining room tables. They displayed the four teen aged girls inside the circle, dressed in their championship uniforms, dribbling a basketball. Standing in the middle of the circle with her four teammates circling around her, was the focal point of the picture…her daughter! She was wearing the number one on her championship uniform, waving to the home crowd, and holding the girls state championship basketball trophy in her hands.

Katie lowered her head, closed her eyes, rubbed the back of her neck, stood up, and moved away from standing directly under the picture. Her neck was hurting already, and she wanted to avoid the risk of hurting it even more by having to hold it all the way back again.

"So that's what they were up to," she said to herself.

She moved to the back of the room, and fixed her eyes again on the object above her head.

They were commemorating their victory, and what a beautiful way of doing it! Katie wondered why they decided to draw their victory picture on top of a ceiling wall in one of the player's bedroom, where only a few will ever get to see it.

"Would not be my way of letting the hometown people know you are the girls state basketball champions," she said to herself. "Pretty picture though, makes you feel like you're right there celebrating with them, wonder which one drew it."

She straightens herself up in the chair, looked up, and noticed the small but legible writing at the bottom and read her daughter's name.

"I should have known," she said smiling, and feeling a bit smug. "Only someone like my daughter could pull off something as spectacular as this."

She looked up at the ceiling again. Then she got up to leave, changed her mind, sat back down, and on impulse opened the desk draw. There was an old black and white school picture of her taken in her senior year playing basketball in her green and gold uniform.

"We didn't win the state championship that year," she said reaching in and pulling out the old picture, and holding it in her hand. "But if we had, and I had a room all to myself and could have drawn pictures like that, I would have probably done the same thing. But I don't think I would have drawn it on top of the ceiling wall!"

She glanced up at the painting and then looked back down at the picture of herself.

"Call me old-fashioned," she said under her breath, as she carefully placed the old picture back in the draw.

Katie then looked around her at all the different pictures hanging on the wall.

"I think I would much rather had just one single picture like this one, hanging on my wall."

She continued standing there amazed and somewhat shocked at the sites surrounding her. Then looked up at the ceiling again and mumbled something about such beautiful talent going to waste. She walked to the window, let the blind back down, closed the door, smelled the rich aroma of the freshly made pot of percolated coffee, and walked back to the kitchen.

Sat down at the table, and was about to enjoy her first cup of afternoon coffee. This was the time of day she had been waiting for. The washing had been done, the furniture dusted off, the floors vacuumed, and the morning rounds to each of the rooms, had been taken care of. Her teenage daughter had left the house to go to the movies. Her nine year old son was in his room, playing with his new Game Boy, and Papa, who she was afraid might be coming down with a head cold, was thinking about going back to bed.

"If all my Saturdays would be as easy as this one," she said to herself, "I might get to work on that book." She let her mind wonder over some of the thoughts hidden away in the back of her mind. 'I have been thinking about writing." She pulled the chair up closer to the table, looked around, as if to admire the work she had done, smiled, and sat down.

Today was Saturday.

No school and no homework for her daughter.

No company to entertain.

This was one of her favorite times of the day—right after lunch, when her family had been fed. The dishes had been cleaned and put away, the table cleared, and Papa had taken an early dose of antibiotics, and had gone back to his room. She leaned back in her chair and smiled. She remembered the child-like pleading in her daughter's voice, this morning, asking her for permission to leave early to go to the afternoon movie.

"I've been waiting a whole week for this movie to show. My friends are taking me in their car," she remembered her daughter saying, just before she left. "Can I please be excused from cleaning my room? The theatre will be packed, and we need to leave early to get a good seat. It's my favorite movie, a love story, and I just have to see it!"

Katie smiled to herself, just thinking about it. She knew about her daughter's favorite movies. She could tell you about every one of them, and how they each affected her. This movie today was no different. Her daughter would come home today in tears, and tell her every little detail of what happen, and then she would wipe her eyes and say, "I wish I had not seen it, it was so sad. The images will stay with me forever."

Then there is her nine year old son. She looked up at his room and smiled. "Ever since she bought him that Game Boy toy, he's been so quiet. I hardly know he's around." She called it a toy, but she really thought it was a miniature computer. "He plays with it from daylight to dark. He takes it with him to his room, and even when he's here with me, he's playing with it. I can hardly believe my own eyes, he's no trouble at all. Getting him that game, was almost as good as winning the state lottery!"

"And Papa," she said to herself, "I don't know what to do about him. Sometimes I think he's as crazy as a lunatic, and other times, he acts like he's got more sense than most politicians I know. I'm afraid he's somewhere right in the middle, and that scares me." She leaned back, and took a deep breath, and continued talking to herself. "I'm blessed I know, but sometimes I think it's a mixed blessing. I have my kids around to keep me feeling young, and having Papa here to remind me that it won't last forever."

She got up from the table, walked to the sink, washed her hands, poured herself a cup of hot coffee, then walked back to the table, sat down, and breathed a sigh of relief. Two loads of washing school clothes, plus folding and separating them, and then putting them away had almost exhausted her. Plus, it had taken up most of her morning. Now it was over. She was finished with her Saturday morning round of housework, and like her daughter, who sometimes waited until the very last minute to do her own homework; Katie too, had put off most of her housework until now. She was now catching it all up at one time, and was almost too much for her. But she had done it. She had washed two loads of school clothes, dried, and folded them.

She has straightened up her daughter's room, made beds, vacuumed the floors, and set up the library room for her daughter's next studying class.

Now she was on her time! She had made it through the Saturday morning rush hour. Now with her daughter at the movies and her son in his room playing with his new toy, and Papa back in bed, she could sit back and 'smell the coffee!'

She could think about that book she had always wanted to write. This was another one of her favorite times of the day. Some people called it 'Tea Time'. Only she didn't drink tea. She drank coffee.

She sat there staring at her cup. The thin dark smoke from the hot coffee, drifted up into her nostril, making her eyes water. The sweet intoxicating smell was making her hyper already, and she hadn't touched the cut to her lips yet. It was a little early in the afternoon to start drinking coffee, she reminded herself. No matter what that article she read last night said about the side effects of coffee, she liked drinking it! It relaxed her, and instead of keeping her awake. It made her sleepy. She remembered what Papa said about going to the bath room a lot, if you drank too much of it.

She dropped her arms down by her side, and let them hang against the side of the chair.

Leaning her head back, she stretched her legs out under the table, closed her eyes for a moment, then pulled herself up, and sat up straight in the chair.

"What the heck?" she mumbled to herself. "I just won't drink too much of it!"

She closed her eyes again, and rubbed them lightly with her thumb and middle finger. Then opened them wide, and reached out and picked up the cup, and swallowed her first sip of what she called her 'afternoon coffee time'.

CHAPTER 3

Katie opened her eyes and the first thing she saw in front of them was a small brown hole on a white tablecloth, and she wondered where she was at. Her head was hurting, and there was a buzzing sound in her ear. She closed her eyes and tried to ignore it, but there it was again. It was more like a ringing sound, and she wondered was it real or was she dreaming. Her face was hurting and her hands were numb. Her fingers were tingling and she felt a stinging sensation when she tried to move them. She lifted her head up off the table, opened her eyes, and looked around the room. She was still in the kitchen, still sitting at the table. Her hands were hurting, and she couldn't move her fingers. She looked down at their ghostly white color, and realized her head had been lying face down on top of them.

"No wonder they hurt," she said. "There's no circulation in them! I must have dosed off!" She opened and closed her hands to get the blood flowing again. She kept rubbing them together and wondering what that buzzing sound was in her ear. Whatever it was, she wished it would go away. It was making her head hurt.

The light was still on in Todd's room and the door was open. She thought she remembered telling him earlier to leave it that way so she could hear him playing and know that he was okay. She could hear Papa snoring from his room across the hall.

"So I wasn't dreaming," she thought. She was awake! The numbness was almost gone from her hands, and she was getting some feeling back in her fingers. "I wonder how long I been asleep? Was it dark outside, or was it still light?" She wondered if her daughter came home from the movies yet. "I must have really been tired," she told herself.

She rubbed her eyes, and looked down at her cup. There was still some coffee in it. She picked it up and put it to her lips. "I couldn't have been asleep too long," she thought. "The coffee is still warm."

She sat the cup back down, squeezed her eyes closed, and grinned her teeth. Then put her hands over her ears, and lifted her head up toward the ceiling. There it was again, that ringing sound, like a bee buzzing around in her head.

"Todd," she called out thinking the sound might be coming from his room, and hopping it was nothing more than the rattling of one of his toys. "Have you been calling me?"

Todd was playing his Game Boy. He thought he heard another sound coming from the front end of the house, but was so absorbed in the game that he didn't pay any attention to it until he heard his mother call his name. Then he realized what the other sound was.

"No," he yelled back. "But someone's been ringing the doorbell. Do you want me to go let them in?"

Katie put her hands down from her ears, wiped them across her face, then stood up and stretched her arms above her head.

"No," she said, bringing her arms to her side and sitting back down. "Find out who it is first, and what they want. Be sure to lock the chain latch, before you open the door."

The boy put his Game Boy down, and ran to the front door. He hooked the chair latch and opened the door slightly and peeked out at a sixteen year old boy standing on the front porch, dressed in a white shirt, leaning against a chair, and getting ready to ring the doorbell again.

"Who was it?" she called out as she watched her son open the door slightly and then close it back.

"It's a boy from the school. I've seen him before, but I don't know his name."

"A boy from the school," she mumbled.

"It's Saturday. What could he be doing here today? Did you find out what he wanted?"

"Yes I did," her son answered. "He wants to come in and talk to an old person. He said he heard we had one living with us."

"Now where did he hear that at?" Katie mumbled to herself. She got up from the table, ran some warm water into the sink, and wet a wash cloth. "He heard we had one living with us, did he," she repeated to herself. "What does he mean by one living with us? Does he think Papa is a pet or something? He must be talking about him. He can't be talking about me. I'm not an old person! But if he wants to get in this house, he'd better come up with a better opening that that.

One living with us, I swear! Don't they teach these kids anything in school about respect for the elderly?"

She washed her face with the washcloth, rinsed it out, wet it again, put it to the back of her neck, and walked back to the table and sat down.

"Ask him why he wants to talk to an old person, and did the school sent him?"

The boy opened the door slightly again then closed it, and ran back to his mother.

"He says he needs another credit to graduate from high school, and talking to an old person is the quickest way to get it, but the school didn't send him here. He said he had to find this place on his own. His teacher told him to talk to an old person, and find out how life was for them, growing up as a teenager, and compare it to how life is for you, growing up as a teenager. He says he's supposed to take a picture of them too."

"That's a pretty tall order," Katie said. "He will have to be a little more diplomatic if he expects to talk to Papa. Even if he is a boy, he still needs to polish up on politically correct English. I don't know about taking pictures. You know how Papa hates to have his picture taken."

"But it won't hurt him to talk to the boy," she thought. "They both might even learn a thing or two from it."

"Tell him to stop ringing that doorbell, and come on in, and you go find Papa, and tell him to put some clean clothes on, and comb his hair and meet us in the Library Room. Tell him to be on his best behavior. He's got a visitor!"

The nine year old boy swung the door open, and let the sixteen year old boy inside the house.

"Don't tell my Papa, he's an old person," the young boy said looking up, and grinning into the older boy's face. "He won't answer any of your questions, if you do."

Katie took the warm wash cloth from behind her neck, rubbed it across her face. She brushed her hair down with her hands, and met them both in the hall, and told her son again to go find Papa. She was wide awake now. The blood was running full force through her veins, and it was hot! She could not believe that a boy had come here, on a Saturday morning, wanting her daughter to help him with his homework. From what her son had just told her, it sounded like the boy standing out there on her front porch right now.

"Needed a lot more than just help with his homework!" she thought to herself.

"Where's Papa at?" her son asked.

"I don't know," she answered too quickly. "I expect he went back to bed. Go look in his room."

The young boy ran off, and Katie led the sixteen year old boy to the couch, and told him to sit down.

"What's your name?" she asked, sounding just as sarcastic as the sour look on her face.

"Robert ma'am," he answered. His voice was beginning to crack up. "Robert Lambert. I'm sorry for the poor choice of words I used when I talked to your son. I'm assuming he is your son, and I apologize for telling him I wanted to talk to an old person. I should have said I wanted to talk to an elderly person.

"That would have been the correct way to put it," Katie said. "And yes, the boy is my son, and thank you, but it's not necessary to apologize. He should not have called you a boy. It is him that should apologize to you!" She leaned down, and stood over him. "You look like a young man, in search of something. Kinda like a reporter, after a story. Wouldn't you agree?"

"Tell me," she said, sitting down beside him, and looking into his eyes, and forcing him to look into hers. "I have both! An old person and a young person. Which one would you like to speak to first?"

The boy opened his mouth to speak.

"You don't have to answer that," she said reaching out and touching his hand, before he could say a word. "It doesn't matter anyway. The young one's not here, and the old one went back to bed, and it would take an act of Congress to him up again!" She moved a little closer to him on the couch. "Forgive me," she whispered. "I'm being a little sarcastic I know, and that's not like me. But we don't usually have students coming out here on a Saturday, and I'm at a lost to figure out why you did." She reached out and raised her hand in front of his face, stopping him again from saying anything, and stood up to leave. "It's alright," she said, turning and walking towards the door. She then stopped and looked back at him. "Look at me," she said, waving her arm. "Now I'm apologizing to you! Would you like something to drink? Of course you would. Wait here. I'll be right back she said, and I'll bring that old person back with me!"

Katie went back to the kitchen, washed her face again with the warm wash cloth she'd left at the sink, then walked back to the table and sat down. "I may as well finish my coffee," she thought. "The boy can wait!"

This was Saturday and her daughter had agreed to help some of the boys with homework she knew, but not on a weekend! Nobody did homework on Saturdays! She got up from the table, and poured herself some more coffee. The boy must not have finished his homework, and wanted her daughter to finish it for him so he could turn it in first thing Monday morning. "This kind of thing happened once before," she recalled, and on a Saturday too! A boy from her school, very similar to the boy sitting out there on her couch right now came here with his sweet-talking, politically correct English, and tried to woo her daughter into writing a report, so that he could recopy it in his handwriting and turn it in as his own work. She remembered her daughter told the boy, "I can't do that!"

The boy then told Papa, his teacher had given him his assignment late, and he had to go out of town on an emergency with his parents for the weekend, and wouldn't have time to write it before he left. Unless he turned it in on the next school day, they wouldn't let him play football.

Papa used to be one of the coaches at the school, and believed the boy. Somehow he got her daughter to write the report for him. She sat back down at the table. This boy was probably trying to do the same thing. But she wasn't going to let her daughter fall into that trap again! If this boy thought he could come here and use Papa to get on the good side of her daughter, just so she would help him get his homework done, whether it was to write a report, or just help him learn to read, he had another thought coming! She'd put a stop to this right now. Her daughter did not do homework on Saturdays, and she wasn't about to start now, and the sooner he learned that, the better off he would be!

She took a big swallow of her coffee and smiled, as she listened to Papa snoring from across the hall.

"I hope he's not in a hurry," she said. "Because if he is, I'm afraid he's in for a long wait! Papa just went back to bed and I don't think he'll be wanting to get back up again any time soon.

CHAPTER 4

The boy pulled himself up to the edge of the couch. He was getting a little nervous. He didn't like waiting, especially in a strange house all by himself with people he didn't even know.

The woman told him to wait on the couch and that she would be right back. She even said she would bring him something to drink. But she didn't come right back, and he was beginning to wonder what he would do if she didn't come back at all. He wished now that he had called first, and asked them if he could come over. If they had invited him here, he might not be feeling so uncomfortable right now. But he was afraid if he had, they would have told him not to come at all. Worse yet, they would have told him to come some other time, and he didn't want that. He'd already spent two days searching for this place, plus another day working up enough courage to ring the doorbell. Now that he was here, he just wanted to get it over with. This was a one-time visit only, and he wanted to keep it that way! Besides, this was school business, so he thought it would be ok with the people living here, if he just came on over. He had told the boy that came to the door to tell his mother he was working on a school project, and ask her if he could come in. He didn't know if the boy told her that or not. Where he lived, he wouldn't have to ask if he could come inside. Everybody knew him. But this was not where he lived.

This was the city! He was a stranger here. This was a big house and two cars parked outside. He didn't know what kind of people lived in this neighborhood. He rang the doorbell four times already without getting an answer, and was getting ready to ring it again. The people living here he decided were either not at home, or just didn't want any company. He didn't want to have to come back, so he was going to try it one more time before calling it quits. He was about to push the button for the very last time, when someone opened the door. This person looked at him briefly, and without saying a word, closed it right back, in his face just to leave him standing there wondering if he should push it again or just leave.

He stood there standing waiting on the porch, while a small boy kept coming to the door, and opening it a little at a time, taking his messages, then closing the door and delivering them back to his mother. They did this for what seemed like at least a half hour. He didn't know what the boy told his mother. The boy finely did open the door, wide enough for him to go inside.

A woman met them both, and told the boy to go find his Papa. She took him to the couch, and sat him down and left him there. Now he was thinking, as he leaned back and prepared himself for a long wait, "They made me wait on the porch before letting me inside the house. Now I guess they're going to make me wait on the couch, before letting me talk to the old person. But I don't mind."

The woman said she would bring the old person back with her when she returned. He wondered that because he had used the "o" word, that she was probably angry and was making him wait here on purpose. He didn't think she looked angry, but she did seem a little upset. He shifted his weight around, and tried to make himself feel more comfortable.

"I wonder who the old person is?" he thought. "Her husband, or her dad?" Then he remembered that the boy said it was his Papa. He ran his fingers through his hair, and rubbed his hand over the back of his neck. "Wonder if Grandma lives here too? He knew some senior citizens lived in this neighborhood. Twice when he traveled this road with his dirt bike, he saw a woman with a senior citizen getting out of a car and going into this house. That's how he found this place!

"So Grandma could be living here too," he thought. "I may have to talk to them both!" He brought his hand down from his neck, and rested it on his lap.

"She's punishing me," he said. "But that's alright. I'm here now, and I don't want to leave.

If she wants to make me wait, then I'll wait. But when she comes back, I won't say that word again. From now on, I'll say senior citizen!"

He lifted his head, and let his eyes move slowly towards the front of the room. "This is a big place," he thought. In the center was a long wooden table with four chairs, and some loose writing paper with scribbled notes neatly spread out on top of it. The area around it was neat and clean. A small empty waste basket was on the floor beside each chair. "I bet the girl that helps students with their homework lives here," he said to himself, as he continued to stare at the table.

"This must be where they do their studying. I wonder if she's here right now? I'd like to meet her, if she is."

Over the past few weeks, he remembered hearing a lot of talk about a girl that was helping some of the boys with their studies. There was nothing strange or unusual about that. Students helped students all the time. That's why study halls were build inside school buildings!

But this girl, as he tried to picture her in his mind, was holding classes at nights, and using her home as the study hall. This is what he had heard about it.

He first thought it was just a friend helping a friend, or maybe a girl helping her boyfriend to get better grades. But word soon got around that this girl was holding classes: two nights a week and already had three boys enrolled. So he thought it very unlikely that she was doing this, just to help her boyfriend. He knew for certain there were students at the school that needed help, and at one time he thought about volunteering to help them himself. But changed his mind, when he found out the ones needing help were all boys, and he wanted to meet girls. He'd never met the girl that was helping these students. He didn't even know her name.

"But if brains and beauty went together...," he pondered. He knew from just listening to the praises everyone at school was lavishing on her. That she could reign as the next beauty queen, and graduate at the top of her class, on the very same night. He heard one boy say that without her help, he might not have stayed in school. He asked a teacher one day, what he needed to do to meet this girl, and get her to help him with his homework. He didn't need the extra help. He wanted to find out if the things he'd heard about her were true. The teacher gave him a number to call, and he called it. But it was a wrong number. It belonged to a girl in a grade under him, and he didn't want to tell the teacher she'd made a mistake. So he threw the number away, and forgot about the whole thing.

He shifted his weight again, and moved back to the edge of the couch. "I wish she would hurry with that drink," he said to himself, clearing his throat, and making a coughing sound. "My mouth is dry and I'm getting tired of sitting here."

He thought he heard footsteps, like someone walking across the floor, and he turned his head to listen. It was coming from across the hallway, maybe from a near by kitchen, or a dining room. It might be coming from the woman that led him to the couch, and left him there. Maybe she didn't forget him after all. Maybe she was coming right now to tell him she never wanted to leave him out there in that empty room all by himself. But something came up, that needed her attention, and she had to leave and attend to it. He cleared his throat and coughed again, hoping that if she was out there, she'd hear him coughing and remember he was still on the couch where she had left him. He hoped that she'd come in and bring that drink she promised with her.

He put his finger in his mouth, looked down at the floor, and felt a little twitch of guilt run thought his body. "I hope she didn't hear me complaining about being tired," he thought. He kept his ears turned toward the sound. His eyes were watching the door, expecting the woman to walk in. But the sound disappeared, and there was only silence left in the room, and his mouth was still dry. He was still sitting on the couch in the empty room, waiting for the woman to come back, and bring him something to drink.

He took a sheet of paper and a pencil from his pack, and laid it beside him on the couch, and looked at the room in front of him. "I've never seen so many books in one place, except at a library," he thought. The room itself was rather large with a closed in fireplace, two reclining chairs, a long table with writing paper, and notes on it, and the big leather couch he was sitting on. A thick white carpet was on the floor and lamps were everywhere. "No shortage of light in here," he thought. Shelves filled with books were all about the room. A small TV and a computer with some more books were on it. In the corner was a shinning new gun cabinet. On top of the cabinet was a picture of a large buck feeding by a river. He wondered if the people living here were nature lovers, or did someone here just happen to like the picture of a deer. "It was a pretty picture though," he thought.

There was a portrait of a middle age woman hanging over the fire place. Looking at it, he knew it was a painting of the woman that had just left him. "She's not as pretty as her picture.

But still, she is a very pretty woman."

Several other pictures caught his eye: one of a small blue-eyed boy; he guessed that must be the boy that had met him at the door when he first came in. And all by itself on a wooden stand, at the other end of the couch cased in a bright gold colored frame was a portrait size picture of the most beautiful girl he had ever seen in his whole life. He sat there motionless for the next moment, just staring at it. Then turned his head slightly toward the door, and listened for the footsteps he so desperately hoped he would hear only a few minutes ago. But now was praying to God, he would not hear them. Not now anyway. Not before he could get up and move to the other end of the couch, and get a better look at that picture. He thought about just getting up and walking to the other end. That would be the simplest and quickest way to get there, he knew. But what if the woman was out there and she heard him moving about in the room? What if she came in to see what he was doing just as he reached the other end, and caught him staring at the picture? What if she thought he was some kind of a pervert, and asked him to leave before he could even get a good look at it?

"I got to get to the other end," he thought. "I got to look at that picture before I leave here, even if she does come in and catch me. I wish there was some way I could tell whether or not she was out there."

He pulled himself up to the edge of the couch. "I'll just have to get up slowly, and walk softly to the other end, and hope she doesn't hear me, and come in." He started to rise up, then thought better of it, and dropped both his arms straight down of his side, and grabbed the cushion beneath him with his hands, and picked himself up, and scooted toward the other end of the couch. He stopped at the end, reached out and took the picture from the stand, and held it up in front of him. She is even more beautiful up close he said, as he relaxed his shoulders and leaned back against the couch. "I'd sure like to get to know her!"

He'd thought he seen her once or twice before, but couldn't remember where. "It must have been in my dreams," he thought as he continued to look at the picture. She was sitting in a lawn chair in a yard beside a rose bush. She had on a pair of white shorts and a dark colored blouse.

Her legs were long and tan, suggesting that she'd recently been out in the sun. He closed his eyes, and pictured himself lying on a towel beside her. She looked to be about fifteen, or sixteen.

She had long red hair and big blue eyes. Her legs were crossed and her chin was resting on her open palm, like she was thinking about something. A freshly picked red rose was lying on the ground near her chair. He couldn't help but think that the rose had fallen out of her hair, and he wondered if that was what she had been thinking about. She did not smile. But her eyes pierced right through him. For a moment, as he continued to stare at the picture, he thought he could get up off the couch, and pick the rose up off the ground and put it back in her hair. "I bet that's her mother," he said, tearing his eyes away from the girl's picture just long enough to look up again at the portrait of the woman. "That boy must be her little brother. The woman said the boy was her son, and the girl has got to be her daughter. They both look like her. I hope she lives here."

He held the girl's picture up near his face and looked suspiciously around the room. Then pulled himself up to the edge of the couch, and reached out and carefully placed it back on the stand. He dropped his arms down, gripped the cushion with his hands, picked himself up, and started his return trip back to the other end of the couch. "Now you can come in," he thought to himself, as he reached the other end and looked up at the woman's painting, and breathed a breath of relief.

"I've seen her picture, so if I don't get to see her here today, at least I'll know who to look for when I get back to school." He put his hands over his mouth and yawned. It was getting late, and he was starting to feel very uncomfortable. He sat up straight again, and his shoulders hurt.

His mouth was dry, and he needed something to drink. He wanted to stand up, and stretch his legs, they were beginning to ache. But he was afraid the woman would come in and catch him standing, and think he was trying to leave. He thought about just extending them out, but he didn't want her to see him doing that either. He squirmed about on the couch. His buttocks were hurting, and his whole body was starting to ache. Maybe they forgot about him. It seemed like he'd been there an hour at least. He looked down at his watch, and it hadn't been nearly that long.

But he'd better start thinking of something a lot more exciting than just sitting here. This waiting was making him sleepy, and he certainly didn't want to fall asleep on this couch. He thought of humming a song, or just thinking about the old person he was going to meet, and what he would say to them. His teacher told him to ask them if they liked going to school, and what they did when their school was out. Did they go on summer vacations, or did they stay at home and go to work? He thought about that for a moment. Of course, he knew the answer to the first question. They would almost always answer with an astounding no! But the truth was most students did like going to school, and he imagined most of them had to go to work when school was out. She also wanted him to find out how they traveled to and from their dates, what music they listen to, what foods they ate, and how they dressed.

He pictured the old person again in his mind. He was pretty sure it was a man he'd seen that day getting out of the car with a younger woman, and coming into this house. The clothes that the person was wearing looked like a man's clothes. He hoped it was a man, but what if it wasn't? He couldn't' ask a woman how she dressed and what she ate, just talking to a woman made him feel uneasy. Asking her questions about herself would make it totally unbearable.

But it was a man, he was sure of that. The woman had told him to wait here, and she would bring Papa back with her. No, he corrected himself, that's not what she said. She said she would bring the old person back with her. What if the old person was Grandma? But the boy said it was his Papa that he would be talking to.

He leaned back against the couch, and stared straight ahead at the wall in front of him.

I wonder what he looks like, he thought, as he turned his head and looked around the room.

And then he saw it! It was a large picture, larger than the one of the woman. The reason he hadn't seen it before was because it was hanging on the wall directly behind him. He had been looking only at objects in front of him. It was cased in a large dark wooden frame, with gold plated lines around each side, only there were no sides. It was round. He couldn't remember ever seeing a round picture. The man in the picture was an old man, a real old man, at least seventy, he thought. He looked mean, real mean!

He had a short white beard and long white hair, and it looked like it had been parted right down the middle. His nose has been broken, and there was a small scar under his lip. Tiny pieces of skin on both sides of his cheek had been removed, leaving little white spots scattered all over his face. His eyes were small and black, and that struck him as being odd. He'd never heard of anyone having black eyes, except after a fight, and he wondered if the man had been in one, and gotten them just before the picture was taken. "That must be the boy's Papa", he thought.

He sat there still staring at the picture and wondering why some of the skin had been removed from his face. "I bet he could tell some stories, looks like he had some rough times growing up. Wonder if he'll talk to me, or tell me to come back some other time."

A voice shouted out from somewhere in the house, and he thought it was the mother telling her son to wake him up. "No, no let him sleep," he prayed. "Don't wake him up." He wanted to shout it out, but he didn't. He didn't want them to wake him up. If the man was sleeping, he could come back and talk to him some other time. If they woke him up now, he would be in a mean mood for sure, and wouldn't talk to him at all. They'd forget about him, and he'd be setting on that couch for the rest of the day.

Suddenly, he wanted to leave. He'd been there too long anyway, he thought. He needed some fresh air. He could slip out the front door. He'd explain to the girl later. She was in his school. He didn't know her, but he'd seen her picture, and he was sure he could find her. But he couldn't do that, he told himself. Someone would notice him leaving, and then the girl would have nothing to do with him later, and he didn't want that. He closed his eyes for a moment.

It would be cowardly of him to leave now. The boy had let him in and the woman had offered him something to drink. She even said he was a nice young man, working on a school assignment. "Like a reporter after a story," she had said. He couldn't just get up and leave now. He wanted to meet the rest of the family, especially the girl!

He pulled himself up to the edge of the couch, straightened his shoulders and faced the hallway. "I will stay," he told himself. "It was just like the woman had said. He was a reporter after a story."

He picked up his pad and pencil. When the woman came back, he wanted to be sitting on the couch in the exact same position he was in when she left him.

CHAPTER 5

"**M**ama, Papa wont wake up." The boy came running back to the kitchen to tell his mother.

He stood in front of her, trying to catch his breath.

"What's the matter?" Katie asked, looking up, and motioning for him to sit down. "Why are you out of breath?"

The boy sat down at he end of the table. "I woke Papa up like you told me to," he said after he had caught his breath. "But it took me a while. I had to keep calling him, and keep wakening him up, cause he kept going back to sleep. I got all out of breath, just trying to keep him awake. I got him up though! But he chased me out of his room! Almost caught me too! He told me to get out, and leave him alone. I told him you told me to wake him up. But he still told me to get out, and leave him alone."

"Ok son, you did good thanks. Papa sometimes gets ill and contrary, when he doesn't get to finish his nap. He may be feeling a little bad too. Do me a favor, and go tell that boy out there on the couch…no ask him if he…never mind. I'll tell him myself. Go back to your room, and do your homework."

"But mama," he said. "Today is Saturday. Nobody does homework on Saturdays. You said so yourself."

"Well go find your sister, and help her. Where is your sister anyway? Why didn't she meet that boy? Didn't she invite him here? Wasn't she going to help him with his homework? Isn't that why he's here?"

"She's gone to the movies mama," the boy said. She said you told her, she could go early today." The boy moved closer to his mother, letting her know he had all his breath back. "I don't think she invited him though," he said. "I don't think he came here to get help with his homework. I don't even think he came here to see her. She would have been here to meet him, if he had. She told you herself, she didn't do any homework on Saturdays, and he didn't act like he even knew you had a daughter." The boy got up from the table and headed back to his room.

He'd been playing a video game about racing cars, and his sister promised to play it with him today, and he wanted to practice so he could beat her.

Katie sat there a few seconds longer, after her son had left. "True," she thought. Her daughter didn't do homework on Saturdays and it was also true that she didn't think her daughter invited him here either. She would know it, if she had. Her daughter always asked her first, before she invited anyone over, and her son was right. The boy did act like he didn't even know she had a daughter.

She got up from the table and walked to the hallway. It had completely slipped her mind that she'd told her daughter she could go to the movies early today. She stood there for a moment, then walked to the end of the hallway, and peeked into the room to see if the boy was still there. He was! He was sitting on the edge of the couch just like she left him.

"He's cute," she thought. "When my daughter sees him, she's going to wish she had stayed home, and met this boy!"

She walked back to the kitchen, poured herself another cup of coffee, and sat down at the table. Even as a child, and in her early school years, as far back as Katie could remember, her daughter was always helping other students with their homework. Since she has been in high school, it has become an almost everyday thing for her to invite some of the girls over after school, to show them how to solve a math problem, or help them study for an upcoming test. At first it was only a few of the girls from her class. Sometimes only one girl would come over, sometimes two or three. They would study as a group for two or three hours, and then go home.

On weekends and when there was no school the next day, sometimes a girl would come over and spend the night, and they would study and play games together and stay up half the night just talking.

She heard one of the girls asking her daughter one night for pointers on how to keep a boyfriend. She turned away and did not hear her daughter's reply. But later she had to laugh to herself at the innocence of both girls, and at the same time, was frightened and alarmed because of it.

But then the girls stopped coming! Her daughter said they didn't need her help anymore.

But Katie knew it was because of what the boys did. A few of them started coming over without permission, and bringing their girlfriends with them. That's when Katie told her daughter that this homework thing had to stop. It did, that night!

Her daughter told her later those boys admitted they were wrong, and did apologize, and promised it would never happen again. A few weeks later, three boys from the school needed help with their homework, and asked her if they could study with her at her house after school, and her daughter asked her if it would be ok. Of course Katie gave her approval!

After her daughter agreed to help the boys, none of them showed up, and for a while, it looked like none were going to show up. Her daughter told her that she thought about reminding them, but she didn't want to seem too eager. Katie told her to be patient and wait. They would come on their own when they were ready. But her daughter told her she wanted to hurry and get started, and she thought about telling the boys that. But in the end decided to take her mother's advice and give them more time.

The very next week, the three boys showed up at her house, wanting her daughter to help them with their homework. Katie met each of them at the door. She wanted to talk to them first, before she let them into the house, and left them alone with her daughter. They all seemed sincere enough she thought, and each one came loaded down with books. The first words out of their mouths were, "Good evening Ma'am. Your daughter is going to help us with our homework." Then they each rushed on into the house.

She talked with each of the boys. She met their parents. She even got to know them by their first name. They were good boys; all three were from her school, two were from her class. They respected her daughter, and most of the time went out of their way to keep their study area neat and clean.

After a while they all become good friends, and sometimes when they had been studying for a long time, and things got real quiet. She would interrupt their studies and tell them its recess time, and bring them a Coke and some cookies that she had baked the night before. Her daughter always liked that. But the boys didn't like the interruptions, but welcomed the coke and cookies.

Sometimes she teased her daughter, calling the boys her in-house dates. They always did their homework in one certain room of the house, and she told her daughter she had named that room the Library Room in honor of her many in-house dates.

Of course none of the boys were her dates. Her daughter was too young to have real dates.

But she had always hoped her daughter would form a close friendship with one of them. She didn't want them to fall in love. They were too young for that! But she hoped a seed would be planted that would grow, and over the years, blossom into a meaningful and lasting relationship. For a while it looked like that might happen.

She liked the boys, the boys liked her, and she knew they liked her daughter. Two hours a night, two nights a week for the past two months, her daughter helped three different boys with their homework. Each boy was getting better grades. Her daughter seemed happy, and the hope she had since the first boy rang her doorbell was becoming a reality. But then the boys became boys! Each one became jealous and suspicious of the other. A rival set in. Each boy started boasting that he was getting better grades, because her daughter liked him better, and she helped him the most. One boy said her daughter favored him, and he got the best grades, because she spent the most time with him. Another claimed that she spent so much time with him because it took so long to answer his ridiculous and stupid questions. Still another boy said they both should just drop out, because her daughter liked him the best, and he was the only one learning anything anyway!

Her daughter didn't seem to mind the rivalry. She thought it was childish, and immature, and it took away some of their study time, since they each brought their petty little issues with them.

But she couldn't stop it, and she wasn't sure she wanted to. She enjoyed the attention it brought her. Her popularity in school was increasing. All her friends were respecting her now, and she liked it. Most of her classmates congratulated her, although she didn't know exactly what for.

She assumed it was because one of the teachers had announced in class that it was an admirable thing that she was doing, giving up her free time to help those boys achieve a passing grade, when they were doomed for an almost certain failure.

Katie took another sip of her coffee, then got up from the table and walked into the hallway, and again peeked into the room where the boy was waiting for her to bring him something to drink. He was still there, just like she left him. She could almost hear him breathing. "But what was he doing here?" she thought, as she stood there watching him. What did he want? Did his teacher really tell him to find an old person, and ask him a bunch of questions about how he lived many years ago? She said to herself, "Well, if that was what she told him to do, he certainly found that old person alright." Right there in her house!

"But how did he know how to find this house?" she wondered. "And how did he find out, that an old person was living here with us? He must have rung a lot of doorbells to find that out! Or did his teacher give him this address and tell him? We had an old person living with us, and our house was the first and only doorbell he rung."

She thought that might be the most likely scenario. She looked at him again. This time she surveyed him more closely. He didn't look like he was here to get her daughter to help him with his homework. He didn't even have any books. His clothes were neatly pressed, like he'd just come from a church. He looked more like the type, that if her daughter needed it, he would be here to help her with her homework.

She sat down in a chair that she'd left in the hallway earlier, and took a big sip of her coffee.

Then got up and moved the chair a little closer to his room, so she could observe him more closely. If he was telling the truth, she thought, and she didn't believe for a minute that he was but if he was, and he just wanted to talk to Papa and ask him some questions, she would help him. She certainly didn't want to discourage him from doing any of his school work. "After all," she said to herself, "it must have taken a lot of courage on his part to go to a strange house, and talk to a strange person. But if he talked to Papa, that's exactly what he would be doing."

She smiled to herself, just thinking about it. "But if his assignment was to go out and find an old person, and his teacher didn't tell him where to go look for that old person, and he had to do all the looking, and searching on his own, then he really did do his homework, and he should be congratulated." She admired him for it.

Looking at him and noticing the determined look on his face she wondered what was she going to tell him. She couldn't tell him Papa had gone back to bed, just to keep from talking to him. That was too cruel. But she had to tell him something. He deserved an answer. She would just have to tell him the truth, and that Papa was feeling bad. She would have to ask him to come back some other time, and she would see to it that Papa talked to him when he did come back. It would be the truth. She picked up her cup, and she swallowed down the last sip of coffee in it.

She still continued to ponder the situation. She wouldn't be telling a lie. Papa did say he was feeling bad, and he did go back to bed, but she didn't think it was because he was feeling bad. She suspected it was because he just didn't want to talk to anybody, especially a boy asking questions about his past life.

Looking at the boy again, she smiled to herself at the thought that was creeping into her mind…she could like this boy! Her daughter would probably like him too. He looked neat and clean.

His hair was combed. Even his shoes were shined, and he had manners, something she rarely seen with the other boys, not that she didn't like the other boys, because she did. She adored each of them, but this boy was different. She couldn't put her finger on it. There was something special about him.

The other boys would always come to her house, with books in their hands, and say, "Good evening Ma'am. We're going to study our homework with your daughter." Then they'd rush on into the house. But this boy, sitting out there on the edge of her couch, just like she left him earlier, waiting patiently, like a little gentleman, waiting for his date to finish getting herself ready for the school prom.

He didn't say anything at all like that. He didn't even mention homework. He just said he wanted to talk to an old person.

When the other boys came over, they were always dressed in their school clothes. This boy was wearing a white shirt and a pair of gray slacks. Of course today was Saturday, so he wouldn't have came from school. Still, she had never seen any of the other boys wearing anything but jeans and a T-shirt.

"But was he telling the truth?" Katie asked herself. "Did his teacher really send him here to talk to an old person?" She didn't think so. He was here to get her daughter to do his homework. She was almost certain of that. He didn't have any book with him. But that didn't mean anything. He probably didn't need them. Most likely, he needed a report written, and couldn't write it himself, and wanted her daughter to write it for him. One of the boys her daughter helped before, must have told him that, when she stopped helping him. He talked to Papa, and Papa talked to her, and she started helping him again. Katie thought for a moment, she remembered that time.

She thought he boy had quit, then changed his mind, and came back. But her daughter told her later, that he didn't quit. She told him to stop coming. Papa told her later that the boy told him, that if she didn't help him to pass this year, he would hang himself in her front yard.

Papa asked him why she stopped helping him in the first place, and after much persuasion, he told Papa that she told him that he paid more attention to his hormones, than he did to his homework.

Papa told him to go ahead and hang himself. Sure enough, two weeks later. He did just that!

Only it wasn't in her front yard, it was in his dad's garage. It was a safe hanging though.

Neighbors said the small piece of rotten rope he used, wouldn't have supported fifty pounds of weight, must less one hundred and fifty. Still her daughter blamed herself, and told Papa she felt responsible, and asked him to call the boy, and tell him to bring his books and come back.

There was still time, and they would study together and if he would apply himself.

She would guarantee him that he would pass.

Katie shifted her weight to the other side of the chair. She knew she had to talk to the boy, and soon too. She had to tell him something, she just didn't know what. But right now, she just needed a little more time. There was something about him that intrigued her. There was something that made her like him. She sat there in the chair, thinking about it. He aroused her sense of compassion. She didn't want to hurt his feelings. She wanted to help him. He worked long and hard to get this interview. She wanted him to have it. If he was behind on his homework, her daughter would help him catch up. Yet, at the same time, he invoked feelings of suspicion, of caution, of intrusion. He wasn't invited here. His intentions didn't seem quiet clear. She didn't believe his story, and at the moment, she didn't trust him.

Did he really think he could come here and win her daughter's favor by talking to Papa?

She hadn't been out of school so long herself, that she couldn't remember what some boys would do to win a girl's favor. So if this was what he was doing, it was a new one on her. It was amusing though, she had to admit to herself. But it wouldn't work. Papa would never fall for it.

Neither would her daughter. She admired him for trying it though. She even thought about playing along with him to see if he could pull it off.

She remembered she had told him she would bring him something to drink. There was some tea in the refrigerator. She got up from the chair, peeked in the room again. She felt a little guilty, picked up the chair, and carried it back to the kitchen, and sat down at the table. "Some cold tea would be fine," she said.

CHAPTER 6

When Kim walked outside the building, and boarded the city bus to take her home, it was raining and she didn't want to get caught out in it. She didn't mind the rain itself, as long as it didn't rain on her. She remembered when she was a kid. She used to sit at home for hours by a window, with the shades pulled up, and listened to it. As long as she was inside, she liked hearing it. It sounded great, and it made her sleepy. Even now, as she listened to it hitting the top of the bus, it sounded good!

But now it was coming down hard, and she was worried that when the bus reached her stop, she might have to get out in it. She didn't get wet when she got on the bus, because the walkway from the building she was in to the bus terminal was covered. But now she was afraid she was going to get soaked when she got off the bus.

Somewhere between when she left the theater and before she arrived home, the rain suddenly stopped, and she was relieved and happy that it had. She had left home this morning without her umbrella, and she certainly didn't want to get wet. Not today anyway. She was feeling bad enough already as it was. Her friends were supposed to pick her up at the theater in their car and bring her home, but they didn't show. She had to take the bus instead and it was crowded. The driver snapped at her because she didn't have the correct change, and that hurt her feelings and now, she just knew when she got home, her little brother was going to laugh at her, because she cried again at the movies.

She got off the bus at her stop, and ran up the steps to her house, opened the door, and rushed inside. The movie had been a little too scary for her, and she couldn't wait to tell her mother all about it. When she left the house earlier today, she thought she was going to see another cute little love story, where boy meets girl, boy marries girl, and they live happy ever after. But it wasn't like that at all! It had a strange and weird ending, and it had her upset and left her in tears. But movies always did that to her. The stories and the people in them were real. She cried at all the movies, and not all were tears of joy.

She liked going to the movies. The trouble was, she put herself into the stories. She played all the parts! They were like an escape to her, although she could not imagine what she would be escaping from. Most to the movies she'd seen were love stories. She liked those the best. They always made her feel good inside, and left her feeling like she could fix the whole world. She liked to imagine herself as the star, and all the good things she was seeing on the screen, were happening to her. She was always falling in love with someone, and all the boys were handsome and rich, and they were all madly in love with her. Sometimes though, the star would die or her love would leave, and she'd rush home crying, only after listening to her sob through ever detail of the story.

Could her mother convince her that it was just a movie? But this particular move that she was coming home from today, was unlike any she had ever seen. It had a very sad ending, and as Kim came into the house, and began to walk down the hallway towards the kitchen, where she knew her mother would be waiting, she was crying and wishing she had stayed home, and spent the afternoon with her brother playing his new video game.

Out of the corner of her eye, just as she was about to leave the hallway and go into the kitchen, she glanced back down the hallway, and saw a boy sitting on the couch in the Library Room, dressed in a white shirt, and wearing a pair of gray slacks.

"Mama," she cried, as she looked towards the table where her mother was sitting. "Who is that boy out there and why is he sitting in the Library Room all by himself?"

Kim had been crying and needed her mother to reassure her that what she'd seen earlier at the movie wasn't real. She wanted her mother to tell her the boy she saw on the screen today didn't really have an incurable disease, and that he was not going to die. When he asked his nurse to dress him in a white shirt and gray slacks and prop him up on the couch, he was simply just an actor playing a part in a move. She needed her mother to tell her again that the boy in the movie wasn't sick. That there was no disease, and no one was going to die! She wanted to hear that it was all just a tale someone had made up, and the people on the screen were just actors playing a part in a story that wasn't true.

But just as she turned, and was about to go into the kitchen and sit down and tell her mother the rest of the story, she glanced again down the hallway to the Library Room and she saw the boy! The door to the Library Room was open, and she could see him sitting at one end of the couch, and he was moving. He did not get up. But he moved, and she stood there and watched.

As he dropped his arms to his side, and grasp the cushions with his hands, and lifted himself up, and scooted towards the other end of the couch. She turned and looked at her mother, then looked back at the boy, just as he reached the other end. She watched him as he reached his hand out and took something from the wooden stand at the end of the couch, and brought it up close to his face. She didn't recognize it at first. Then as he slowly and carefully put it back on the stand. She saw that it was a picture. Her picture!

He had been looking at her picture, and he was smiling and at that moment, as she watched him place the picture back on the stand. She forgot about the other boy she'd seen at the movie, with the incurable disease. She wasn't at the movie anymore. She was home now, and she was not crying. And there in her house, was another boy, and he was waiting for her. And she was thinking of him now.

Her mother had just told her that he was in the Library Room, and she seen him out of the corner of her eye. When she came home from the movie, and he was wearing a white shirt and gray slacks, and he wasn't propped up on the couch about to die. He was sitting up straight on the edge of her couch, and this was not a story. She wasn't watching a movie. This was real, and her mother was saying that he wanted to talk to someone.

"Come sit down dear," her mother said breaking Kim's consultation on watching the boy.

"You can tell me all about the movie, And I'll tell you all about the boy and why he came here.

Kim walked into the kitchen and stood looking at her mother for a moment, then brushed her hair out of her eyes, and sat down at the table across from her. She and told her all about the movie. She told her how sad it was, and how she cried thought almost all of it. She told her how the boy with disease and he knew he was going to die, and asked his nurse to put a white shirt on him, and a pair of gray slacks and prop him up on the couch one last time, and let him wait for his mother to come home.

Katie reached out and touched her daughter's hand. "Look sweetheart, "she said, "You have a chance now, to relive that movie, and give it a happier ending." She reached her arm out and pointing towards the room down the hall where the boy was waiting. "There is a boy out there, sitting on the couch, just like your boy did, and he is dressed in a white shirt, and gray slacks.

But unlike your boy in the movie, this boy is not sick!" She was pointing her finger in the air to emphasize her point.

"On the contrary, he is very anxious to talk to someone, and you should go out there and talk to him, and bring him something cold to drink, and try to cheer him up. He came here wanting to talk to Papa. But Papa wouldn't talk to him, and I don't know how to tell him that."

Kim listened to her mother talk for a few minutes longer. Then got up and walked to the refrigerator. Got out a can of Coke and turned and started walking down the hallway, leaving her mother at the table. Still wondering how she was going to tell the boy that Papa had gone back to bed, and wouldn't talk to him, she continued walking hastily toward the room where the boy was waiting. She was walking too fast and there was no need to, but she wanted to. Her mother said he needed to talk to someone, and she was going to talk to him.

She was entering the room now. She could see him sitting on the couch, waiting for someone. Just like the boy in the movie did. She could hear his slow breathing, and smell the starch in the white shirt he was wearing, and for a short moment, she wondered if he was sick, and she closed her eyes and prayed to God that he wasn't She should slow down, she told herself. She was almost upon him. She didn't want to startle him. She wanted to talk to him!

She wanted to tell him she was sorry he had to sit out there on the couch for so long by himself.

She was going to tell him she had something cold for him to drink. Her mother said he'd been waiting a long time. She wanted to tell him she had come home now, and he wouldn't have to wait any longer.

She kept walking towards him and she should stop now. She was standing in front of the couch where he was sitting. She could reach out and touch him. She hadn't realized, she had been walking so fast, that an inch closer, and she could have touched his feet with her own.

She should move back. She didn't want him to think she slipped upon him, but she stood there looking down at his legs dangling over the edge of the couch. He had his head down, looking at the floor, and didn't see her. He looked tired. Her mother said he was cute, but he was more than just cute. He was handsome!

His shoulders were broad and muscular, and he was tall too, she noticed, and the clothes he was wearing were just like her mother had said.

"He must have come straight from a church. A church in heaven!" she said under her breath, as she made the holy cross sign of thanks in her mind. And all of a sudden standing there so close to him, she wanted to reach out and tell him to come with her to the kitchen, and together they would talk to Papa. But she didn't say a work. She just stood there looking at him. She wanted him to look up and say something. But he just sit there, looking down at the floor.

She reached out her hand, and her mouth opened, and the words came out. It was just a whisper, and she quickly put her other hand over her mouth. But it was too late.

She didn't want to ask him that question. She was thinking about it, but she didn't mean to say it. It just came out. It was more of a statement, than a question, and soon as she said it, she regretted it. But she couldn't take it back. She just hoped he didn't hear it. But he did!

"Do I have a what?" he shouted back, without looking up. The question shocked him. It was such a strange and unusual thing to ask. He didn't mean to shout, and he would apologize later.

But right now, all he could think of was the woman had came back, and she had brought him something to drink, and he would have the chance now, to stand up, and stretch his legs, and none to soon too, he thought. They were beginning to cramp.

He looked up, and saw the woman standing over him, and she was leaning down, and holding something in her hand, and she was close. Too close, and he thought. He couldn't stand up now. If he did, his body would hit her body. As she fell into him, and both their bodies would fall to the floor, and he remembered thinking. This was not the woman that left him sitting on the couch and told him she would be right back, and would bring him something to drink. This was the girl he wanted to meet! This was the girl he'd seen in the picture sitting in a chair by the rose bush, and she was young and beautiful, and her hair was long and red, and she was bringing him something to drink. He wished he had the rose to give to her to put back in her hair. And he remembered where he'd seen her. It wasn't in his dreams, it was at a basketball game!

She was playing, and he was in the audience. Her team had won, and had gone on to win the state championship. The school's paper had devoted all its coverage the next day to the accomplishments of the team, and had praised its star center. A full size photo of each of the first team players accompanied the writing, and he recognized the center as being the girl in the picture sitting in the chair, by the rose bush. She didn't look that tall he thought, but now, looking up at her, he could see that she was tall and she was falling, and it scared him so he tried to sit back down.

But it was too late. He was already standing. The Coke can fell from her hand. His arms instinctively reached out and grabbed her around her waist and pulled her to him. Her body pressed tightly against his own, both her arms wrapped around his neck. Their bodies clung to each other, and for a short moment, they both stood there, locked in each other's arms holding each other up. Then they fell to the floor and he was on top of her, and she screamed.

CHAPTER 7

Todd was playing his computer game with his ear phones on when he heard the scream. He quickly pulled the ear phones off, and rushed out of the room to see his mother and his sister both kneeling down over the boy, who was lying on the floor. Papa was standing over him, with an aluminum skillet hanging down from his hand.

"He's coming to now," Katie said, as she begin to rise up off the floor. "Back up, and give him some air."

"He was just knocked unconscious. He'll be alright," said Katie.

"Get him a glass of water, Todd," she said. "And hurry!" She stood up, and watched her son run off towards the kitchen.

Katie knelt back down on the floor, beside the boy, and leaned over close to him.

"Do you feel like getting up and sitting on the couch," she asked, looking into his eyes. "I know it's not your favorite place. But right now, it's a lot softer than sitting here on the floor!"

She smiled and reached under his arms, and helped him onto the couch. Todd returned with a glass of water and handed it to his mother.

"Here drink this," she said, holding the glass out to him.

"What is it?" he asked, shaking his head and trying to get his eyes to focus.

"It's that something to drink, I told you, I'd bring you," she said smiling. "It's just water," she added. "It's what you need right now." He took it and drank all the water, then handed the empty glass back to her.

"Thanks, he said, I'm feeling better now. But how is the girl, is she alright? I didn't want her to get hurt. I was trying to keep her from falling, when I lost my balance."

"I know," Katie said. "I saw you holding her. You both looked so cute, holding on to each other. If I'd had a camera, I could have taken a picture of it, and you could show your friends how you two not only met by accident, but even caused the accident you met in!" She laughed, and patted his hand. "It's ok," she said. "You broke her fall, and that saved her from getting hurt, and I'm grateful to you, and I'm sure she is too."

Katie moved next to him, on the couch, and told him to be still. "The girl is fine" she said. "She's here with us now. She wasn't hurt at all, thanks to you. You can talk to her later. Now give me your hand, and let me check your pulse."

She placed her finger on the radial artery on his wrist, and looking at the minute hand on the watch on her own wrist, began mentally counting his heart beat.

"Your pulse is fine, she whispered, 74, just about perfect. How does your head feel?"

"Like it hit something hard, when I fell," he answered.

Both the boy and the girl who had hastily moved to the other side of the room, just moments ago now moved back in close, and sat down on both ends of the couch. Papa, who had been standing over him when Katie told them all to stand back and give him some air, had left and gone back to his room.

Katie moved even closer to him and motioned for her daughter to come closer too. "Does your head still hurt?" she asked. "Do you want an aspirin?"

"No, it's stopped hurting now. The pain is completely gone," he added.

"Are you sure?" she said. "You want a doctor to check you over?"

"Yes," he said. "I'm fine, and no, I don't want a doctor to check me over. I just don't know why my head hurt so bad all of a sudden in the first place."

"Papa hit you on it!" The girl spoke up. When we both fell, you landed on top of me," she continued, "and before you could get off me, Papa came in and saw you, and hit you on the back of the head with a skillet."

The boy lifted his head, and saw the girl sitting not far from him on the couch.

She looked up, and met his gaze. They stared at each other for a moment and they both smiled. Then he dropped his head, and looked down at the floor.

"She is a hundred times prettier than her picture," he thought. "Why didn't I talk to her before when we were alone out here in this big room?" Then he remembered. He wanted to, but he didn't get the chance. Just as he began to stand up, and get off the couch, she suddenly appeared from out of nowhere. She was there standing over him, leaning down and holding something in her hand, and as he rose to meet her. She fell into him, and then they both fell.

He smiled to himself. But before they hit the floor, he caught her in his arms and held her, and it felt good! She had both her arms around his neck, and was holding on to him, even as they fell.

Just thinking about it, made him forget the bump he felt on his head.

He looked up, and caught the girl looking at him. She smiled, and he smiled back. He pulled himself up straight on the couch, and continued looking at her. Just meeting her, he thought to himself, was worth getting hit on the head!

Katie looked at her daughter, then back at the boy. They both seem to be lost in each other's gaze. She reached up and snapped her fingers in front of the boy.

"Ha," she said looking straight into his eyes. "If I could get your attention for one moment, I'd like to introduce the rest of my family to you. She stood up in front of the boy, and looked towards the end of the couch, where her son was sitting. "Thank you," she said smiling, and walking down to the end of the couch. "This is my little man, Todd." She rubbed her hand over his head and patted him on the shoulder. "You met him at he door, when you came in. Remember? And my name is Katie," she said looking at the boy and walking back towards him.

She sat down on the couch beside the girl.

"And this girl sitting here beside me, that you keep staring at is my daughter Kim." She reached out and squeezed the girl's hand. "But I think you already met her!" She smiled, and looked directly at the boy. The boy smiled back, and stood up. Then looked embarrassed and sat back down.

"And you said your name was Robert," she continued. "I'll get Papa out here in a few minutes, and you can meet him. And then we'll all know each other, and he can tell you why he hit you on the back of the head, when you were down on the floor."

Katie, Kim, and Todd stayed in the Library Room, talking with Robert after he had regained consciousness. Katie explained to him what happened, and told him, she was sorry for not trusting him from the beginning. She told him her daughter was not home when he first rang the doorbell or she would have met you at the door herself, and you would not have had to wait outside so long, and she added with a grin.

"I was a little upset at you myself. I thought you came here to get my daughter to help with your homework. Like that other boy did last year when my daughter did return home. I told her you were in the Library Room waiting to talk to Papa, and I asked her if she would go talk to you because I knew Papa had gone back to bed, and it would be much later when he got up again. I was trying to find a way to tell you that myself too. I was afraid, if we didn't tell you something soon. You might get up and leave. I knew Kim would be tired from her bus ride home, and I wasn't sure she would talk to you, or if she would go directly to her room and go to bed. So I followed her into the Library Room. If she had gone straight to her room, then I was going to talk to you, because I wanted you to know that Papa was feeling bad, and I was going to ask you to come back tomorrow, and I would see to it that you got to talk to Papa.

"After I was satisfied that my daughter was going to talk to you, I was going back to the kitchen, and give you two a chance to get acquainted. I was about to turn around and leave the room when I saw Kim walk up to the couch, where you were sitting. She leaned down, and said something to you. I couldn't hear what she said. But I could see that when you looked up at her and that you were startled. I don't know if it was because she was standing too close to you, or if it was because of something she said."

"I do know that, just as you stood up, she leaned down, and I saw both of you lose your balance, and both of you began to fall into each other, and I watched as the two of you met in mid air and then I saw you somehow regain your balance and remain on your feet, and you reached out and grabbed her around the waist and pulled her to you, and she had both her arms around your neck, and was hanging on for dear life. And then you lost your balance, and both of you fell to the floor, and you landed on top of her, and that's when Papa heard her scream, and came running into the room."

She looked up at Robert, and shrugged her shoulders.

"With my daughter laying underneath you, well, you can see what kind of an impression he got, and he grabbed the first thing he could get his hands on, which happened to be an aluminum skillet hanging in the hallway right outside the door, and ran towards you, and hit you on the back of the head with it."

"I apologize for what he did", Katie said. I hope you understand why he did it. It was one of those impulse things. But at the time, he thought it was the right impulse to follow. He's very protective of his granddaughter, as you now know. But he is a good man, and I know, once you've met him, you'll think so too. If you will stay for dinner, you can meet him and see for yourself. I'll explain to him what really happened, and he will apologize to you himself."

Robert said he held no bad feelings toward Papa. In fact, he added that he was glad it happened the way it did. He smiled. If that skillet was a picture, he'd like to frame it! He told them that he was sure that he and Papa would get along just fine and he'd like to stay for dinner, and meet him.

But it was getting late, and he was a little tired. He looked at her, and patted his head, then quickly added, "My head isn't hurting though." But he thought he'd better get on home, while he still could. There were some things he needed to do before it got dark, and he did want to get to bed early tonight, because he wanted to get an early start tomorrow. He needed to go into town, and if any of the stores were open, he wanted to buy a present. But if he could, and he looked straight at Kim as if he only needed her permission, he'd like to come back tomorrow, and maybe she'd go to the movies with him. He continued looking at her, and moved a little closer toward her, and smiled.

"Would you to the movies with me tomorrow?" he asked.

Kim opened her mouth to answer, and moved to the end of the couch. Katie jumped up and moved in between them, before she could say anything. "Why yes, Robert. That sounds like a good ideal," she said. "Why don't you come back tomorrow, and you and Kim can go to the movies together, and I'll make sure Papa will be here, and out of bed too, and he'll apologize to you."

"Yes come back tomorrow, Kim said. "And come early, and I'd love to go the movie with you. That is the least I can do! I could have hit my head on something, or injured my spine when I fell, and be confined to a hospital bed. Or have to have someone push me around in a wheelchair for the rest of my life. If you hadn't caught me and held me up long enough to break my fall...how can I ever thank you?"

She raised herself up off the couch, and looked at her mother, then sat back down, and turned her eyes to Robert, smiled and moved a little closer towards him. He stood up, and walked around her mother to the other end of the couch, where she was sitting.

Sat down beside her, looked into her eyes, and reached out his arms and smiled.

"Go to the movie with me tomorrow," he said.

CHAPTER 8

They stood there, the three of them looking at the blank stare on each of their faces, waiting for the other to speak first. Robert had left and Papa was still in his room. Katie looked at her daughter and smiled, letting her know that everything was alright and she wasn't angry and then started walking towards the kitchen.

"It's all going to work out fine," she said breaking the silent, and motioning for them to follow her. She reached out and jokingly grabbed Todd by the ear. "Don't be teasing Kim about that kiss either," she said holding his ear, and gently leading him into the kitchen. "It was just one of those "So-long-see-you-later-type kisses anyway. Probably didn't mean a thing! Besides, she is old enough to let a boy kiss her, if she wants him to." She was looking over at Kim. She looked back at Todd and saw the puzzled look on his face.

"I know what you're thinking," she said. "Papa would not have allowed it, if he'd been here, and I wouldn't have approved of it either" Katie went on still holding onto Todd's ear. She glanced over her shoulder and smiled at her daughter. "If I'd know it was going to happen…but I didn't see it coming. I don't think any of us did, not even your sister. I don't think he really planned on doing it himself. But when your sister said that she'd go to the movie with him and I told her she could…then I hugged his neck and invited him to come back tomorrow…and then Kim told him to come early…I think he was just overcome with joy, and so happy at being accepted. It came over him that when Kim walked him to the door and told him good night, he just forgot himself and reached out and kissed her."

She let go of Todd's ear and glanced at Kim and smiled, then motioned for them both to sit down.

"You reckoned he lost some of his senses," she said leaning down and whispering in Todd's ear. "After all, you got to remember, he was hit on the back of the head with something!" She stood up and winked at Kim and then leaned back and hugged Todd's neck.

"Just kidding," she said rubbing her hand roughly through his hair. She took two Cokes from the refrigerator, and poured herself another cup of coffee. "You're sister wasn't hurt," she said rubbing Todd's head again. "And Robert didn't do anything wrong. Except maybe kiss your sister in front of all of us." She glanced at Kim, noticed the blush on her face, then looked back at Todd.

"I think your sister is wanting us to change the subject," she said taking a swallow of her coffee, getting up, and moving to the end of the table.

"But I still don't understand," Todd said following her with his eyes. "If Robert did nothing wrong, why did Papa hit him on the head with that skillet?"

Katie sat her cup down on the table, and looked apologetically at her daughter and then got up and moved back beside her son.

"I thought I explained that part to you once," she said. "But I guess I need to explain it one more time."

She got up again from the table, pushed her chair in, and walked to the other side, and sat down facing him. "I was in the room with them," she said, looking straight into his eyes. "I saw what happened! Kim walked up to the couch where Robert was sitting, leaned down over him, and started talking. He was expecting me to come back, and didn't see her come in, because I told him before I left that I'd be right back. He told me later that his legs and buttons were hurting him so bad, from sitting in one place for so long that when he heard a woman's voice, he was so overjoyed and happy because he knew I had came back, and had brought him something to drink, and now he would get the chance to stand up, and stretch his legs.

Katie looked directly at her daughter sitting across the table from her, and reached out and took her hand.

"It was only then, when he began to rise up off the couch. That he looked up, and saw her falling into him, that he realized it wasn't me," she said turning loose of her daughter's hand, and looking again at her son. "Then as I stood there unseen by both of them. I saw Robert catch her in his arms, and hold her up for a moment, and then he lost his balance, and they both fell. She screamed when they hit the floor, and that is all that happened. Papa was already up, and out of his room and almost to the kitchen, when he heard the scream. That's how he was able to get to her before you did. I believe he was coming to tell me he was ready to talk to the boy. Of course, I was not in the kitchen. I was in the Library Room, but he didn't know that. In any case, he rushed into the room when he heard the scream. He didn't see me, all he saw was your sister lying on the floor with Robert on top of her. No one was hurt, and like I told you before, it was an accident. Papa didn't see what really happened. He only saw what he thought happened!

But I'll let him tell you about that. He's in his room. Why don't you go get him? Tell him to come to the Library Room and we'll meet him there. We need to talk! He needs to tell us all, just what he thought he saw."

Papa met Todd at the door to his room, and told him to tell Katie he had lain down, went to sleep, and would need a few minutes to wash his face, comb his hair, and wake himself up before he would be ready, but he would be there shortly. He encouraged Todd to go on back, and stay with Katie. He handed him the skillet in case that boy came to, and tried to run away.

"You may have to hit him on the head, and knock him out again to keep him there until the police arrive." Papa closed the door to his room and walked back to the closet, and laid out a clean pair of pants and a shirt. This time he wouldn't need Katie to tell him what to wear. He would surprise her. He would put on some clean clothes, comb his hair, and maybe even wear a tie.

After all, the police would be out there waiting. They needed him to tell them just what happened. He had to look respectful didn't he, if they were going to believe him? But then again, how could they not believe him? It was quite obvious! The boy tried to rape his granddaughter right there in the Library Room in broad open day light. "He was a strange boy," he thought shaking his head. "He probably has a record a mile long! The police would probably tell him they should not have let the boy in the house, and they would have been right!" He had warned his daughter time and time again, about letting strangers come into the house.

He parted his hair down the middle, and tucked his shirt tail inside his pants. "I'd better hurry," he told himself. He didn't want to keep the cops waiting. It was obvious to him now.

Katie had called the police. Why else would she send Todd to his room to get him? The boy didn't say they were out there, but he did say that Katie wanted him to come, and explain to us all what he saw. That was proof enough for him, since he was the only one that saw what happened. Why else would she say for him to explain it to us all if there weren't more people out there? They needed him so they could finish making out their reports. He was sure of that!

They were going to congratulate him; they might even give him a metal or put his name in the paper for preventing a crime. But just in case they haven't arrived yet, he told himself, he'd better get on out there, especially if that boy gained consciousness. Katie would need him, and he sure didn't want them to be alone out there for any length of time with that crazed boy.

CHAPTER 9

"Looks like we're going to have another clear, cloudless day," a woman's voice said from inside the radio. "A little cool this morning, with some wind from the north, but later on there will be plenty of warm sunshine."

Papa rolled over, thought about pushing the snooze button on the clock radio beside his bed and going back to sleep. But he remembered telling Katie he would be down for coffee early this morning, and as much as he wanted to stay in bed, listen to the weather report, and let that smooth talking voice put him back to sleep, he told himself that he better not push that button.

He best just get up right now, this very minute, and turn her off before she said another word or he would be drinking coffee at his table this morning all by himself!

"Not a cloud in the sky," the voice continued as he rose, found the knob on the radio, and turned it off, cutting the woman short before she finished giving her report.

"The makings of a beautiful day," he thought as he dragged himself out of bed and got out his only clean shirt and clean pants. He had left them hanging in the closet, and laid them across a

71

chair. He trimmed his beard, took a shower, got dressed, brushed his hair down with a brush someone had left in his room, and looked at himself again in the mirror. He could hardly believe it himself. He was dressed up in a white shirt, and even wearing a tie! Man, was Katie going to be surprised!

She was always saying that he refused to comb his hair, without her threatening him first.

Well he'd show her he could dress up, even if there was no real reason to. Besides he did have a reason. But even if he didn't, he could always say it was Sunday, and that was reason enough.

He even thought about telling her he wanted to go to church. But he'd better not push his luck.

She sure enough would think he was sick if he told her that!

He was hoping to get to breakfast early enough this morning to see Kim and Todd before they finished eating, and find out a little more about what really happened yesterday. He wanted to apologize to her for any wrong doings she thought he might be guilty of. He knew he had been wrong in his judgment of Robert. Katie had made that clear to him last night! But he still wasn't too sure about the boy's intent, and he wanted to talk to Kim and see how she felt about it. He had counted on getting to the table while she was still there, and telling her how bad he felt. Now that he knew the truth about that boy, he could beg for her forgiveness, and find out what he could do to make it up to her.

He would and drink some coffee while he waited for them to eat their breakfast. But instead, he got there just in time to see them both leave, and all he got was the usual exchange of good morning greetings, and neither one of them said anything about him, or what happened yesterday, or what was said about it last night.

"Must have stayed in the shower too long," he grumbled to himself as he watched them go into their rooms. "Well at least she didn't seem hostile towards me, and that is a good sign," he thought, as he pushed his chair up closer to the table and sat down. Katie came in and laid a large shopping bag down on the table beside him. She said good morning, opened the blinds at the window, and brought him a fresh cup of coffee. She then turned and left the kitchen to go finish making up a bed that she had started earlier. She said she would be right back, and would be happy to sit down and drink some coffee, and chat with her "all dressed up man" at his table.

Papa straightened his tie and thumped off some dirt from it.

"So she did notice," he thought as he watched his daughter leave. He started to get up and say something, but changed his mind and pulled his chair back a little further from the table. He closed his eyes and let the bright warm sunshine gushing through the open blinds warm his face.

Despite what she had told him last night about how wrong he had been, and how he had over reacted to everything, he was feeling good!

He was just going to sit here, and drink his coffee, and soak up as much of that warm sunshine as he could, as he was sitting just there waiting for her to come back, and tell him what really happened. He told himself that he may as well be thinking of what he was going to tell her when she came back. He knew that she was going to ask him if he could accept the fact that the whole incident was just one big accident. By accident, he figured she meant the coming together of that boy and his granddaughter and the remark she mentioned previously about him approaching that boy from behind, and hitting him on the back of the head. Although she hadn't said it yet, he was sure that she would just as soon as she came back from making up that bed.

"My one big accident," he mumbled to himself as he swallowed some more of his coffee. "One of many I made that day, more like a ton of them," he thought. When the alarm first sounded that morning, he should have pushed that button, and went back to sleep. But he had to admit, Katie was right. What happen between that boy and his granddaughter was an accident, and nothing more. He realized that now, and by him waking up, leaving his bed, and going to the kitchen to tell Katie, he knew that he would talk to the boy.

That was an accident too! Everything that happened to him that day was an accident...him getting up after going back to bed. Even now, he couldn't believe he really did that. Why didn't he just play sick and stay in bed and let Katie wait on him the rest of the day? And that boy, coming here in the first place that was an accident too! How in the world did that boy pick him to talk to out of hundreds of other senior citizens scattered all over the county?

And any other time, his granddaughter would have been all tired out. When she came back from the movies, she usually would have gone straight to her room and onto bed, especially since she had to ride home on a crowded city bus. The one time in six months, he decides to dress up, and go to the kitchen, and have coffee and breakfast with his family...the only clothes he had clean...and ready to wear was his white shirt and a pair of gray slacks. The exact same kind of clothes that boy was wearing, when he showed up here yesterday.

"That couldn't have been a coincidence," he said looking down at his coffee cup. "It had to be an accident! You just don't plan things to happen that way. That boy is a stranger to us and to this neighborhood...coming here unannounced, and sitting in a room all by himself...for almost an hour after waiting outside on the poach before getting into the house, and then being left alone...on the couch after being told someone would be right in to talk to him...one would think he'd get up and leave, but he didn't. It's like he didn't mind the wait. And then, Katie leaves him out there on the couch all by himself, until her daughter comes home from the movies…and then she sends her into the room where he's at…she tip-toes right up to the couch where he is sitting, without letting him see her at all, and leans down over him, and reaches her hand out, and says something to him. He looks up, shocked and surprised at seeing her standing there."

"But thinking finally, someone has come to talk to him, and now he can stand up, and stretch his legs, and meet her at the same time. He begins to stand up, and as he does so, she leans further down, loses her balance, and begins to fall into him. He reaches out and catches her in his arms, and somehow they stand there for a moment or two, holding each other up, he looses his balance, and they both fall. She screams. I hear the scream, and fearing she is being attacked, I rush toward the room, and seeing them both lying on the floor with him on top of her, and thinking the worse has happened. I grab the first thing I see, which happens to be an aluminum skillet hanging by a nail on the wall in the hallway, just outside the door. I run in and hit the boy on the back of the head with it."

"Now you tell me," he said looking at his almost empty coffee cup, "how could all these events be happening at the same time without somehow being connected? Are they accidents or merely a coincidence?" He continued to stare at his cup, as if expecting it to answer him.

"Katie washed clothes that day too," he said. "She usually washes all the clothes when she does the laundry." Why didn't she wash any of his? He picked up his cup and swallowed the last drop of coffee in it, then sat it back down next to the shopping bag. He'd have to remember to ask Katie about that.

Katie came back into the kitchen, picked up his empty cup, refilled it at the sink, stopped, and stood looking at him for a moment. Then went over and sat down beside him.

"You look nice," she said with a big grin, as she handed him his second cup of coffee. "You should dress up more often, it makes you look...well younger. But its seven o'clock in the morning! "What's the occasion?"

"Oh, no reason, just felt like it," he said.

She looked at him as if he was sick or something, then got up, and smiled. "Well you look good anyway."

"Thank you. I'm glad you noticed. But right now, I'm not feeling that way."

"Oh," she said turning around and looking back at him. "What makes you feel like you don't look good? Are you sick?"

"No," he said looking up at her and trying to smile.

She walked back to the table and leaning over and looking at him she said, "Well, I can think of two very good reasons why you'd come to breakfast wearing a white shirt and a tie, and neither one of them is because it's Sunday. One is that you look good. The other is because you want to look good. So which is it? I've told you three times already, that you look good, but you say you don't feel like you look good? So that leaves me to believe you got all dressed up in those clothes, because you wanted to look good! Who did you want to look good for? I've already said, that I thought you looked good!"

He picked up his cup, put it to his lips, made a frown like the coffee was bitter or something, and then sat it back down on the table. "Do you think Kim will ever speak to me again?" he said as Katie brought her coffee to the table and sat back down.

"Of course she will. Why would you think she wouldn't?"

He bowed his head and looked down at the floor. "Because of what I did to that boy, and what I thought he did to her."

"Oh don't be silly," Katie said. Kim liked the fact that you took up for her, and Robert said if he'd been in your place he would have done the same thing. It's like I told you last night. You did what you thought was right, and it was right, and I'm glad you did it. I'm proud of you, and Kim is too."

"I don't know," he said without looking up at her. "It looked to me like she was in a big hurry to leave when she saw me coming to breakfast this morning.

Katie picked up her cup and looked at him without saying another word. "So that's why he's all dressed up," she thought. "He thinks Kim is mad at him, and he wanted to look good for her. He thought coming to breakfast this morning all dressed up in his best clothes would impress her. Pretty smart thinking, I'd say. I knew he didn't get all dressed up for nothing! He knew Kim would eat breakfast early this morning, and he thought if he was here too, she'd have to talk to him. And I know he told me he'd be down early, but I never dreamed it would be this early!

I didn't think he could get out of bed before six o'clock on any morning. He waits till the kids are about to leave for school before he even comes down on week day and he never gets out of bed before nine on weekends. He is here sitting at the kitchen table, all dressed up in a white shirt and a tie at seven o'clock on a Sunday morning. If I didn't know better, I'd swear he wanted to go to church!"

"Don't be so sensitive," she said, as she sat her cup back down on the table and smiled at him. "Kim will always speak to you. You're her Grandpa. It may take a little time before she does, but she will eventually speak to you. She has to! She lives in your house, and she has to tell you good night! Just kidding." She laughed.

"I'm sorry Papa, that was mean of me and I apology." She smiled and reached out and grabbed his hand. "Of course she will speak to you again, she has never stopped, so don't be thinking she has. She left the table early this morning because I told her to. I told them both to leave as soon as they finished eating, and go straight to their rooms, and do their homework, and anything else that needed to be done, so they would be free for the rest of the day, and could get to bed early tonight. Got to get up early tomorrow, school day you know!" "Robert is coming over, and he wants to meet you and take Kim to an afternoon movie; although, I did tell him to come early and eat dinner with us. I made it perfectly clear to both of them that they had to get the okay from you before they could leave the house together. This is your granddaughter's first date Papa, and you're responsible for making it happen!"

"What do you mean I'm responsible?" Papa said. "You saying it's my fault that boy's teacher sent him here to talk to me."

"No," Katie said. "I'm not saying that at all. I'm just saying if you had talked to him when he first came here, like I wanted you to instead of going back to bed this would have never happened, and he wouldn't be coming back here today. I would not have gone to the Library Room where he was waiting, and told him a little fib, or rather a big fat lie, and he would have left and went home. And just maybe he would have come back some other time. But chances are he would have gone someplace else, and that would have been the last we'd seen of him. But now, thanks to you, he's coming back! Only this time it's to see Kim, not you. But no, you had to change your mind and get up out of bed, and head for the kitchen to tell me that you decided to talk to him. But it was too late. I wasn't in the kitchen. I was already on my way to the Library Room to tell him that little white lie, and ask him to come back tomorrow. Because I thought you really were feeling bad and had gone back to bed, and wouldn't be able to talk to him. But don't worry Papa, I'm not blaming you."

"I'm actual glad he's coming back. It's like they were meant to meet, regardless of what we did anyway. Cupid just shot a couple of his arrows, and one hit that boy, and the other hit my daughter, and neither one of us could have done anything to prevent it, even if we had wanted to.

But now what are we going to do? He'll be here in a couple of hours, and he wants to take Kim to a movie. I can't tell her she can't go, since I told her last night she could, and we can't go with them, because they won't let us. I could tell him that old person he came to see yesterday, was out of bed now, and would talk to him. But this time, he's not here to talk to an old person.

He's here to take our daughter out on a date! You could tell him, he could save his money, by staying here, and not going to a movie. But he's not thinking about saving money either. I told Kim it would be nice if she stayed home, and spend her first real date in the Library Room. But she said they wanted to see a movie. I even told her, I didn't have any money to give her for the movie, but she said that's okay because she'd ask you for some. So cheer up Grandpa, rest assured, she will speak to you again!"

CHAPTER 10

Katie let go of Papa's hand, picked up her cup, smiled at him, then got up and carried it to the sink. She then walked over to the cabinet, got out her new silverware and china dishes, and carefully sat them down on the table, and reached into the shopping bag and pulled out the new table cloth and the four new chair pads.

"I went back into the store yesterday and bought these right after I got the coffeepot," she said. Looking up at Papa and seeing the curious look on his face, she knew what his next question was going to be: "When did you get those?"

"I got another white tablecloth too," she said holding it up and showing it to him. "It blends in good with the curtains, just like the old one did. The chair pads are red, wait till you see them. They match the color of the chairs, and their so soft to sit on. After you and I eat our breakfast, I want to put them on the chairs, and put the new dishes and silverware on the new tablecloth. Then set the table for dinner. We'll eat early tonight, right after the kids come back from the movie."

Papa lifted his head and looked up at her. "I liked the old tablecloth. What was wrong with it?"

"The small hole the spark burned in it was getting to be a big hole," she said, "and I didn't want Robert to see it."

He stood up, put his hands in his pocket, took them out again, and sat back down. "Not to change the subject," he said, "but I think I'm going to like this boy. He's a little like I used to be...sees what he wants, and goes right after it! He just met Kim here yesterday, and now he's coming back already to take her out on a date. Even in my younger days, I wasn't that fast! You think we can trust him out with our little girl? I mean, we don't know what kind of a person he is. Shouldn't we run a back ground check on him first?"

"That's why I invited him here for dinner," Katie said, "to do just that!

There won't be enough time to do just that, if they go to the movies," he said. "And after their gone, we won't need to do just that! Wasn't Kim supposed to stay at church and practice something today?" he asked.

"Yes," Katie said. "A Christmas play or something...I had forgotten about that, and I bet she did to. She needs to be there today too. It's their first rehearsal, and she told me herself that she wanted to be a part of it."

"Well, instead of her going to the movie with him, tell her to ask him to go to church with her," Papa said. "If he says he'll go, then we'll all go together, and at least we'll know he's not all bad. And if he wants to leave after church, he can leave with us, and even come home with us, if he wants to. But if he wants to stay at the church with her during the rehearsal, and watch her act, then I guess we'll count that as his back ground check!"

"Brilliant thinking Papa!" Katie said. Him going to church with her is a great start towards winning our trust. You're getting smarter by the minute. I'll go tell her right now just to be sure and tell him as soon as he gets here. Does that mean you'll be going with us too?" she asked.

"If I can wear what I got on," he answered. She looked at him and smiled.

"I guess you can, but I thought you might want to chance into something a little less noticeable."

"Well I would," he said, "but in addition to the two reasons you gave me earlier, for wearing these clothes there is actually a third reason. It's the reason I'm dressed this way."

"Oh," she said, "and what reason is that?"

He pushed himself away from the table, and walked over and stood beside her.

"You didn't wash any of my clothes yesterday, and I didn't have anything else clean to put on."

CHAPTER 11

"**G**ood to see you in church today," the pastor said, as he stood in the doorway and greeted Katie and Todd on their way out. "Glad you brought your family with you and a visitor too I see. Your family is one of the few that do show up early, every Sunday morning, and I appreciate that. Some of our members have been coming in a little late, I regret to say. I shouldn't complain though. They have their reasons, I'm sure.

Katie smiled, as she let go of his hand and watched out of the corner of her eye, as Robert was standing right behind her and Kim was not too far behind him. She stood waiting in line to take her turn to meet the pastor and shake his hand.

"Enjoyed your message," she said as she grabbed Todd's hand and turned and walked outside to wait for Papa.

"Welcome young man," the pastor said as he shook Roberts's hand. "I hope you got some good out of our service today, and will come back again as often as you can."

"I did and I will," Robert said. The pastor smiled and let go of his hand, and began shaking the hand of the next person waiting in line. As he walked outside, Robert thought of the times when his mother used to take him to church as a small boy. He watched as Papa and Kim waited to reach the front of the line, and take their turn at shaking the pastor's hand. He too sometimes would stand outside the church with his mother, and wait for a friend or a visitor who had gone in with them, but for some unknown reason, chose not to sit with them. When the service was over, they had either left their seats late or had somehow got caught up in the rush for the front.

Just like Papa; they too had to wait in a long line to shake the pastor's hand before they could exit the building.

Robert walked outside the door, and saw Katie leaning against her car and started walking towards her.

"I wish Papa would come on out too, so I could leave," she said. Trying not to show her frustration, as she met him she took his hand and led him back to the car. "I just hope he doesn't make me wait too long. I wanted to get home early and start dinner. You didn't happen to see him on your way out, did you? I guess what's taking him so long, is that everyone in front of him wants to talk to the pastor and shake his hand."

She looked down at her watch and murmured something to herself. She then let go of his hand and leaned against the car.

"I hope you don't think I'm always this impatient with him," she said looking up and smiling. "But he does try my patients at times. Every time he comes with me, and I want to leave as soon as church lets out, something like this happens. Either he has to wait inside for someone else to use the bathroom before he can use it himself, or on his way out, he gets stuck in line behind some little old lady who has quite a story for the pastor. She will go on about how her forty-year-old son who is still living with her is running around with a nineteen-year-old school teacher, who she thinks is married to a policeman that lives next door. She's afraid that if he doesn't stop carrying on with this woman, he is going to get himself into a lot of trouble, and she wants to know if he can tell her if there is anything she can do to put a stop to it. At least, that's what Papa tells me! Sometimes I think he just makes those things up to create an excuse for himself. I keep telling him that if he has to sit up near the front, to get up out of his seat, and get in line as soon as he hears the last "Amen" and then get in the line to shake the pastor's hand so his wait in line won't be so long. But he won't listen to me."

"Most of the time, church has already started or just fixing to when he goes in, and he has to sit wherever he can find a seat, and that usually is up front with a friend, or a visitor. Then when church is over, it takes him a long time to get out because he stays in his seat too long, or just stands around and talks with anybody that will listen, and I end up standing outside waiting for him, and having to talk to someone I really don't want to talk to. I know five or ten minutes doesn't sound like a long time to wait for someone to come out of church, but you're not supposed to go there just to socialize either. Anyway, it's not the waiting that really bothers me so much, it's the reason for it! I've told him over and over, that we all go in together. We all go sit together, and we all get up and leave together. But for some unknown reason, he wants us to go on in, and him stay outside, even when there's no one out there to talk to. If I didn't know him so well, I'd swear he just wanted to stay outside to smoke a cigarette. But I guess he figures since we arrived a little early and church hasn't started, he can hang around outside until it does.

"The trouble with that is he always finds someone out there to talk to, and before he realizes it, church has started, and when he does go inside, he's late! I'm afraid when the pastor made that little remark earlier to me about some of our members coming in late, he was talking about Papa. Next time, if he doesn't go in and sit with us, I'll tell him to sit near the back, so when church does let out, he can be among the first to leave the building."

She looked up at Robert and smiled, and leaned against the car, beside him. "I know you sat with Kim and me today, and I'm glad you did. Kim is thrilled that you came with her. I hope you didn't mind us sitting near the back. That's where I like to sit. I'd sit on the back row every time, if I could, but I can't. Their already taken, before I get there! I should have asked you where you wanted to sit, before we went in but I forgot. So if it's alright, I'll ask you now." She moved away from the car, then walked back, and stood beside him.

"When you go to your church," she said looking up into his face and smiling, "where do you like to sit?"

Robert close his eyes and thought again of his mother. She was a good church-going person. They both were. If going to church qualified you as a Christian, which he knew it didn't, but if it did, he thought his mother would be one of the best Christians around. Every time the doors opened, she was there, and she always brought him with her. She didn't socialize much while she was there. She shook the preacher's hand on her way out, and sometimes told him she benefited from his sermon, but never said she enjoyed his message. "That sounded too much like the preacher had entertained her," she used to say.

He rubbed his eyes with his fingers, then took his sunglasses out of his pocket, straightened them over his nose, and leaned beside Katie against the car. "When I went to church," he said looking away, then looking back at her. "I was always with my mother, and the only thing I remembered was that we went a lot, and I was never allowed to sit with anyone but her." He pushed his glasses up with his finger and looked straight into her eyes and smiled. "But to answer your question, she liked for us to sit near the back. If I had a church to go to, that would be my choice too."

He took the sunglasses off, and put them in his shirt pocket. "And to tell the truth, before this morning, I hadn't seen the inside of a church since I last went with her, and that was quite some time ago. I wanted to go back. I really did, but without her there to go with me, well, it was just so easy to stay home or go someplace else. I guess I just got out of the habit of going. Mother always told me a person shouldn't go to church merely because it was a habit, but if that did happen, it was a good habit to get into. I guess going to church with her was just a good habit I got into."

Katie looked up at him and smiled, then opened her purse felt around in it, closed it, smiled again, and reached out and squeezed his hand. "It sounds like your mother was not only a wise woman, but a very good mother as well. Wait here a second, I got to get my glasses." She walked to the side of the car, opened the door and got her sunglasses off the front seat, and put them on. She looked at herself in the mirror and walked back, and leaned against the car beside him.

"I thought for sure Kim would have followed you out, since she was standing right behind you. I'm surprised she let you out of her site, much less to come out here all by yourself. I guess she got out of line and stopped to talk to someone or Papa asked her to wait inside with him while he used the bathroom, which is probably what happened."

She put her arm inside his, and leaned against him. "It looks like neither one of us will be going anywhere anytime soon anyway because I have to wait for Papa to come out before I can leave, and he obviously is in no hurry, and you have to wait for Kim. But don't worry, she won't leave you out here for very long at a time, I'm sure of that," squeezing his hand again and moving her arm out from under his.

"It was out of the question for me to think I could leave early anyway," she said looking away from him and trying to stay calm.

"I don't know why I even thought I could, in the first place. But I can't blame it all on Papa. I would have had to wait anyway. I wanted to stay and say a few words to Kim, before I left." She let go of his hand, looked up at him and smiled. "At least this time while I'm waiting, I get to talk to someone I really want to talk to!"

She turned and started walking towards the other side of the car. "So why don't you put your sunglasses back on," she said looking back at him. "And let's wait in the car, and you tell me what else your mother said."

Robert closed his eyes and opened them again and smiled, as he sat down next to her in the car. He let his mother's words run across his mind. He remembered how she would patiently go over each procedure with him before they left the house.

"Well for one thing," he said as he leaned over a little closer to her. "My mother liked to prepare for everything. And preparing for church was just about as serious to her, as being ready was." He lowered his gaze and staring down into Katie's face like an FBI agent might stare into the eyes of a suspected criminal while the interrogation was going on, "it was a way of doing things, a set or rules to follow!

"We need to get to church a little early today," she used to tell me. "And be seated before the other members arrive, especially since it's a Sunday morning. Because I'm afraid if we don't, it will be so crowded with the new preacher visiting and all. It may take us most of the afternoon just to get out of the building!" She would always say, "We don't want to sit on the very back row when we get there. We couldn't anyway even if we wanted to. The mothers with small babies already have them sewed up! But we do want to get as close to them as we can."

Katie put her hand over her mouth, cleared her throat and looked up at him and grinned. "Your joking aren't you? Your mother didn't tell you that?"

"No," Robert said taking his sunglasses out of his pocket, and putting them back on.

"I'm not joking! She told me that, and a lot more!

"And when she told you that they already had them sewed up, she meant the back rows were reserved for mothers with small babies?" she asked, taking her hand down and clearing her throat again.

"No," Robert said. "My mother didn't mean that at all. The back rows weren't reserved, anyone could sit in them. But no one wanted to challenge a young mother, with a couple of crying babies on her lap, and besides, I think everyone figured they should get to sit there anyway, in case they had to get up and leave the building in a hurry, or get to some other little room when their babies started to cry. And they would cry, you could count on it. I think everyone agreed they really did need to sit close to the exit, so they wouldn't have to walk so far when they did have to get up and leave. They were always getting up to go somewhere, either to the bathroom, or to some other place close by. Babies do tire easily, and cry a lot when they have to stay in one place. It is very distracting to hear someone's baby crying in your ear, especially when the singing is going on, or the pastor is making a special announcement, and you want to hear every word he's saying. You just can't tell babies to stop crying and expect them to obey you, and you can't let them keep on crying either. So the mothers do get up a lot, during the service, and take them outside, and sometimes they have to be in a big hurry to get them outside too."

"And I guess the members that would have liked to sit on the back row, like myself, I just got used to seeing the mothers with small babies there all the time, and realized they needed them more than we did, and just left them alone. We never bothered sitting with them, unless of course the church was full and those were the only seats available. My mom probably felt it might be a disservice to the mothers in the church if she didn't say that. Her being a mother herself, made it easy for her to understand and defend what the mothers with small babies in the church had to put up with. They didn't want to cause a distraction, and I know, they don't like disturbing other members, so when their babies cried, they get up as quietly as possible, and leave the building or go to another room near by, and stay there as long as necessary. Not just to keep the others from hearing the noise their babies made, although that was the main reason, but also to keep the good members of the church from getting mad at them, and spreading rumors that their babies might be catching a cold or something. 'It was true,' my mother said."

"They did miss out on some of the worship, and social activities at the church especially at nights when the services were a little long, and their babies were tired and sleepy, and the mothers had to keep getting up out of their seats, and taking them outside, sometimes for extra long periods of time while the pastor was preaching, because the babies wanted to go home, and to bed. I'm sure my mother would tell you, if she was here today. Those mothers would much rather have stayed in their seats, and heard the song that someone had sung or listened to the details of the special announcement the pastor had made, instead of getting up, and having to leave while it was going on, and then having to hear a watered down version of it from some distorted member who never wanted to hear it in the first place."

Katie balled her hand into a fist, put it over her mouth, and cleared her throat again. 'Sorry to interrupt you," she said, forcing him to stop, and look at her. "But I just have to tell you. I am so pleased to hear you speak so highly of your mother, and in such a notable and admirable way. It says a lot about you. I didn't know her, but from you're amusing and humorous ways of describing her views and beliefs, I feel like I've known her for years! Sitting here listening to you so vividly tell of her sound wisdom, and diverse ways at getting things done, is very interesting. The way she finds answers to some of life's little problems that confronts each of us from time to time is simply amazing. The way you so brilliantly tell how she solves each of them is also very entertaining Instead of wishing Papa would hurry and come out, so I can go home, I find myself hoping he stays in there longer so I can stay here, and listen to you tell how your mother, so boldly, and in such delicate matter. But it does leave me wondering about the size of the church she took you to. I'm not a fan of big churches myself, I prefer the small and simple ones. Their much easier to get in and out of so I'm guessing the church you and your mother went to was a small country church, like a camp meeting, or maybe a tent revival where everyone knows everyone," she said, looking up at him and trying to smile. Or was it a large church where unless your introduced to the person before you sit down, you won't even know who's sitting next to you?"

She smiled, turned her head away, and then looked back at him. "It makes me wonder if a lot more churches around here, including this one, might benefit from your mother's clever and unique seating agreements."

He pulled himself up on the seat, and looked straight ahead. "Why is Kim staying in there so long," he asked, looking back at her. Then turning his head, and watching a couple come out, and get into their car, and leave, "Why hasn't she already came out? You think I should go back inside, and look for her? Maybe she's waiting for me to meet her in there."

"No," Katie said. "She called me on her cell phone, while I was in the car, and said she'd be a little late, and asked me to stay with you. She said the Youth Minster needed to see her, something about a change in schedule. Papa is with her now, and its about time for his football game to start, and he definitely won't be late for that. So don't worry, she won't be too much longer. I should have told you right after she called, but I forgot, please forgive me."

She pulled her sunglasses off, wiped her eyes, then put them back on, and looked up at him and smiled. "You and Kim may get to go to that afternoon movie after all! But right now, before she comes out, tell me about that church you and your mother went to. Was it one of those big mega churches? I always wanted to go to one of those myself."

"No," he said. "It wasn't a big church at all, and not a whole lot of people went to it. But still, there was a good many that did, and quite often visitors would come, and my mother would tell me that by sitting near the back, you could see who the visitors were without turning your head around, and avoid embarrassing yourself, as well as maybe frightening off the visitors. Because most of the time she would add with a big grin, they would walk up your isle, and choose a seat in front of you anyway. As a visitor would walk in after church service had already started, and someone seated up front, or anywhere for that matter, would turn their head around, and look back, he/she often would continue to stare at the visitor until they had found a seat. She said he knew he had told her about this a few times before, but felt the need to keep reminding each of the members, that it was a very rude thing for anyone to do, and he encouraged all his members not to do it. They not only take the chance of embarrassing themselves the pastor would tell her, but he would also add that they also run the risk of causing the visitor to feel uncomfortable, and insecure of themselves, especially if small children are with them. Not to mention the damage it could possibly have on the church itself by causing the visitor not to want to come back again."

"I guess," he said, "it was one of those things, some people did on impulse or without thinking. Even though, I'm sure at the time they did it, they knew within themselves, they wouldn't want it done to them. Of course, she told me she wasn't ever guilty of doing it herself, and made me promise to remind myself not to do it, if I ever found myself even thinking of doing it."

"She was asked onetime by a church member, if she ever wanted to visit another church. Yes, she'd thought about it, and she told the other member that she'd like sometimes to go, if for no other reason, but to see how they worshiped. Of course she added that she was curious to see if anyone she knew went there, but she told me that she told the other church member, she never would go. This was because the pastor at the church she was thinking about visiting was rumored to nearly always ask his visitors to testify or to dismiss the service with a short prayer. She didn't want to embarrass herself. She just never was very good at saying prayers in public."

"Here comes Papa now," Katie said looking a Robert and opening the car door. He looks confused and lost. He probably forgot where we're parked. We better get out, and stand against the car, so he can see us. Otherwise he might wonder around for hours looking for us."

Papa saw them leaning against the car waving their hands and realized he was going in the wrong direction, turned, and started walking towards them. "Kim said for me to tell you that she had to go see Brother Bob," he shouted as he came near them, "and for us to go on home, and for Robert to wait for her in his truck."

"No need to shout," Katie said as she walked up to him. "I can hear you just fine. Stand here against the car and catch your breath, and tell us what else she said."

Papa leaned against the car, rested for a moment, then rose up and rubbed his hand across his chin. "That was a long walk, almost tired me out," he said. "I don't know why you had to park the car so far…"

"What else did she tell you?" Katie said pointing her finger at him and showing her impatience.

"She said to tell you that she would be out in ten minutes. That the church play has been cancelled, and that her and Robert would leave here together, and probably go straight to the movies." He leaned back against the car, hesitated a moment, looked at Katie, then back at Robert.

"That is if he still wants to take me," he added. He moved away from leaning against car, stood up straight, shrugged his shoulder, looked at Katie, and smiled. "She told me to tell him that too."

CHAPTER 12

"Do you want to go to the movies?" Robert asked looking at the girl sitting beside him. He was smiling as he left the church parking lot, and drove his truck out into the highway. It had just started to rain, not hard, just a light drizzle, and he wondered if he should turn his lights and wipers on.

"I don't even know what's playing," he said as he continued to look at her, then quickly turned his head and looked back at the highway in front of him. "But it was the only place I could think of when I asked you to go out with me," he continued. "I wanted us to go someplace where we could be by ourselves." He turned the lights and wipers on, glanced again at Kim sitting beside him, and reached out and touched her hand.

She felt his touch as she heard him ask her about the movie and say he wanted to be alone with her. She wanted to be alone with him too, and it pleased her to hear him say he wanted the same. She felt his hand, and squeezed it lightly. A warm tingle radiated up her spine, and a bright red glow covered her face.

"Not really," she answered, lifting her head and looking at him and then looking back at the highway. "I know it's about a man who takes his girlfriend on a date, and ends up driving her down a dark country road where he rapes her, then kills her, and buries her in the woods, and I don't think either one of us wants to see anything like that," she said looking back at him. "But it is where I told mama we were going and I don't want to feel guilty when I get home for telling her we went someplace else."

"I know, Robert said glancing back at her. And you won't because when we tell her what was playing, I think she will be rather pleased that we didn't see it! Besides, you didn't tell Papa to tell her we would go to the movies. You told him to tell her we would probably go to the movies! But if we don't," he said slowing down, and grabbing the steering wheel with both hands and turning off on a country dirt road, "where will we go? "Just before your mother left the church, she made me promise to have you home by six o'clock."

Kim leaned back against the seat, and stared at the dirt road in front of her. She saw no other traffic, only thick woods on both sides of the two-way street. And she thought of what could happen to girls who let boys take them down lonely dark deserted roads like this one. They come back expecting to have babies, and sometimes they don't come back at all, she remembered her mother telling her.

Robert took his hands off the steering wheel, raised his arms high in the air, let out a yell in a sudden outburst of emotion, then brought them back down and looked at her and smiled.

"You know what that means," he said wiggling his body a little closer to her. "That means since we're not going to the movies, we'll have about five hours all to ourselves to mess around, and do just about anything we want to before I have to take you home. So tell me my sweet, what would you like to do? We can do anything you want to! Is there some special place you'd like to go? We can do that too," he said looking at her and leaning over and bumping her playfully with his shoulder.

"No, no special place," she said looking up at him and smiling. She laid her head on his shoulder. "You're driving, and I'm your passenger. I hope to be your wife someday, but right now. I'm just your girlfriend, and I want to go wherever my boyfriend wants to take me."

He laughed and slowed the truck down. "Well then," he said slowing the truck down even more. "I know where we can go, and kill a couple of hours, and still be back at you house in time for dinner, and its not too far from here either."

"Good," she said. "I will go anywhere with you my darling, but before we start, can I ask you where we're going?"

"Yes of course you can," he answered reaching out and touching her hand. "You will always have the final say so in such matters."

"Great," she said lifting her head up then laying it back down on his shoulder. "Then tell me my dear. Where is my boyfriend taking his girlfriend?"

"To his place," he said looking at her and smiling. "It's just a short ride from here and I think you'll like what I have in mind."

"Oh I don't know about that," she said lifting her head off his shoulder and quickly sliding to the other end of the seat. I do like you very much, and at some future date, I want so much to become your wife, but until that future date comes, I'm just your girlfriend, and this girlfriend is not going to make love to anyone, except her husband!"

He slowed the truck down, pulled off to the shoulder, put the engine in park, and turned to face her. "I like you very much too," he said. "And I want to be your husband."

"I want you to be my husband," she answered. When you are my husband, I will make love to you!"

He moved out from under the wheel, and turned his body to face her. "I respect your feelings," he said. "I honor them, and as much as I would like take you in my arms, and make love to you right now, I will not, and I wasn't taking you to my place have sex. I was taking you there to meet my dad! He saw your picture in the paper playing basketball, and that's his favorite sport, and when I told him I knew you, well, he wanted to meet the girl who led her team to victory and brought us the state championship. I was going to induce him to you."

She moved back a little closer to him and reached out and grabbed his hand. "I'm sorry," she said. "I thought you just wanted to. . . ." She stopped and looked up at him and began to cry.

"Don't cry," he said putting his arms around her. "You'll mess up that pretty face. We'll just ride around for a while, and then go back to your place, and help your mother with dinner."

She sat there for a moment with her head bowed, then dried her eyes with her free hand. "No we won't "she said looking up at him and smiling. "Mother doesn't need our help, and we don't have to go back right now. I know just what we can do, and have fun doing it," and she added sliding back beside him. "I know just the place where we can do it! It's what I want and I think it's what you want to." She took his hand, and put it on her leg and placed her hand on top of it.

"We'll go to your place," she said moving up close to him and smiling. "I'll meet your dad!"

He looked at her like she had just waked him up from the pleasant dream he was having.

The expression on his face changed from a glowing red to a pale dark pink, and she knew right away from just looking at the frown on his face that he knew she was the one that had awaken him, and she could see that he was not happy about it! She wanted to tell him that she was sorry, that she didn't mean to upset him and that she really did want to go to his place, and meet his dad. But he looked angry and hurt and she was afraid if she said anything else, he would be mad at her and she didn't want that.

Suddenly, he pulled his hand back, moved his legs all the way out from under the wheel, looked at her, then reached out, and took her in his arms and kissed her lightly on the lips. All at once, she relaxed and she wasn't afraid anymore. She felt content, and at ease cuddled in his arms, feeling his lips moving over her mouth, knowing he still liked her and wasn't angry. She felt safe, sitting next to him in his truck, parked on the side of a country road, enjoying his lips on hers. She answered his kisses with her own, and as he pulled away from her, and moved back under the wheel to turn the ignition off, and lock the doors to his truck, she remembered thinking about what they had been doing. "Kissing and necking," her mother called it. "It was the very first thing a man and a woman did when they dated each other and that was alright. But if they continued to date, there was a second thing they could do and that wasn't alright!" Her mother would go onto to remind her, "Because after they did that, they usually didn't want to date each other anymore. It made them want to do, one of two things. They stopped dating altogether, and start living together or they got married, and then started living together, which is what your dad and I did!"

As Robert finished kissing her lips and moved back beside her, she began laughing and shaking her head from side to side, as he slowly ran his lips over her ear.

"That feels good," she said. She was shaking her head. "But it tickles."

"That's what you get for teasing me," he whispered. "Now you're going to pay!"

"So that's what he was upset about," she thought. She closed her eyes, and pressed her ear further against his lips. "He thought

I was teasing him." She remembered putting his hand on her leg, and telling him we'd go to his place. "I guess maybe I did," she thought to herself as his open lips continued to brush against her. Then she felt a soft tender bite, and her head went back, and she let out a little yell. As his tongue went inside her ear, and her body went limp as he slowly pulled her down on the seat beside him. She felt her body explode as he slowly unbuttoned her blouse, and slowly rolled her over on her back. She opened her mouth, and let him touch her with his tongue.

It was the first time she'd ever done that She had heard other girls talking about it, and seen men and women kiss that way at the movies, but she never imaged herself having any part of it.

She always thought it to be unclean and distasteful. But now, she found herself putting her tongue on his and moving it around in his mouth. It felt natural and she was enjoying it. He was moving his hands over the upper part of her body, and she felt them gently pressing against her breast, and it felt good. No boy had ever done that to her before, and she found herself liking it, and it made her feel good inside knowing that he was liking it to.

She lay still on her back, feeling the weight of his body on top of her. His lips brushing lightly against her neck, and then slowly moving down her open blouse, and she thought that this kissing and necking thing was rapidly coming to an end, and what her mother called the second thing was about to begin. She knew it was going to take her places, she'd never been. She opened her eyes, and felt his hands on her breast, and watched as his lips moved further down her body, and she knew he wanted to take her to those places, and just for a moment, she closed her eyes, and wondered what it would be like, if she let him.

Then she remembered what her mother said happened. Once this second thing occurred, and she knew she didn't want to stop dating Robert, but she also knew for certain, they were not going to start living together, not now anyway, not before they were married. His lips were wet and sweet, as they continued their descent on her body. His hands kept pulling tenderly on her breast and she knew where he was going. She knew she had to stop him before he got there. She felt his hands unbuttoning her blouse exposing her naked skin. She rose up and watched him kiss each of her breast. She knew if he didn't stop this thing from happening right now, she wouldn't be able to stop it from happening later, and by then, she doubted if she would have wanted to.

"There's only one thing left to do," she said out loud looking at him and hopping he would hear her. "We got to get married! So we can start living together, and then this second thing can happen as often as we want it to." She reached down to pull him up, and move his hands from her breast. But they were already gone, and he was buttoning up her blouse. He had already pulled himself up, and was laying over her. Looking down into her eyes, she looked up and saw the look on his face. He rolled off her body and lay still on his side, and she knew. He must have seen the look on her face and heard the words she had said. He had stopped on his own, and she was pleased, and yet a small part of her knew that if he had not stopped when he did, she wouldn't have cared if he had not stopped at all!

She turned over on her side and lay facing him. "Thanks," she whispered as she kissed him and put her arms around his neck.

"For what?" he said. "I didn't do anything."

"That's what I'm thanking you for," she said. "You didn't do anything, and that was the best thing you could do, and I love you for not doing it." They both rose up and sat straight on the seat facing each other and he took her in his arms and kissed her.

"I love you too" he said, kissing her again lightly on the cheek and brushing her hair away from her eyes. He put his hand under her chin and lifted her face up until she was looking straight into his eyes.

"I saw that look on your face and I heard what you said. 'Not until we are married,' you said, and it reminded me of what I said. I would not make love to my girlfriend and you are my girlfriend!"

Their lips met again and his arms held her a little tighter. Then slowly but gently he pushed her away. He reached out and took her hand and squeezed it. He put his finger on her lips.

"I'm telling you right here and now. I will make love to her, once she becomes my wife!"

They sat there in the truck for the next few minutes, parked on the side of the road holding hands waiting and not saying a word. They just sat there looking at each other. And in those few silent moments, they both knew that there was something there they could not see, but something they each felt. Something happened that would change their lives forever.

"I want to spend the rest of my life by your side," Robert said.

"And I want to spend the rest of my life being by your side," Kim responded.

She reached out her hand and put her finger on his lips. "Don't say another word," she said.

"Let's just go to your place, and meet your dad!"

CHAPTER 13

Robert stopped his truck on the concrete driveway in front of his house. He turned the lights and wipers off and then turned and looked at the girl sitting beside him. Normally on a clear day when the road was dry would have taken him about ten minutes to complete. Today the road wasn't dry. It was wet and the wet stuff kept coming down making the dirt road a hazard for anyone to drive on. The rain had been falling lightly all over the county for the past two days.

But the rain was not enough to keep the people living in the cities where the roads were already paved from driving to church or interferer with their daily activities. For people like Robert and his dad who lived in rural areas, where some of the roads had not yet been paved, it was more than enough to keep the roads wet and muddy, causing them to become slippery, dangerous, and unsafe to drive on. This forced Robert to drive slow and cautiously, turning his ten minute drive to his father's house into a thirty minute ordeal. On this particular afternoon, with Kim sitting in the truck beside him, he was driving extra careful. This was not the time for him to be a hero, and show off his driving skills on a wet dirt road to his new girlfriend. He wasn't afraid of getting stuck in the mud; he knew how to avoid that. He was concerned about going around a curve too fast, or hitting the brake too hard, and sliding off the road into the ditch, and damaging his truck. And now was certainly not the time to leave his vehicle parked in a garage somewhere waiting to be repaired before he could drive it again. He needed that truck to be running…when the most beautiful girl he had ever seen in his whole life would be riding in it with him.

He shut the engine off, stretched his legs out under the steering wheel, then reached out and took her hand.

"Sorry about that rough ride," he said looking at her and smiling. "For a moment back there, when we were rounding that curve, I thought we'd have to call a wrecker to come pull us out of the ditch. But we didn't thank goodness," he said reaching out his hand and touching her shoulder. "Hope this rain stops soon so the road can dry and we can get in and out ok. The county's been talking about paving our road for years, and now rumor has it, that sometime next year they're finally going to get around to doing it."

He took the keys from the ignition, put them in his pocket, and moved a little closer to her.

"You sure you want to do this?" he said. "You don't have to, you know. There's no real hurry.

We can go someplace else first, and then come back here later. It doesn't have to be done now."

"Yes it does," she said. "I really want to do it. I just hope it's not too soon." She slid over toward the door. He jumped out, and hurried to her side, opened the door, and helped her out

She took his outstretched hand.

"I hope he likes me," she said putting her other arm around his neck.

"Oh he will, I'm sure of it. He'll probably hug your neck, and may even kiss you. If he does, don't think anything about it. That's just his way of greeting someone he likes, and believe me, he's going to like you!"

He walked the short distance from the truck to the walkway in front of her, guiding her steps, and keeping them off the wet grass. He then stopped, took her hand, and together they both skipped up the three steps leading to the front door.

"Knock, knock. I'm home" he said as they both walked across the front porch and knocked lightly on the door. He glanced at her and pulled her closer to him. "I've got someone with me. Someone you'll want to meet, and she wants to meet you too. I hope your dressed causes we're coming in.

Robert pushed the unlocked door open, took Kim's hand, and walked in. "Dad," he called out as they both walked down the hall toward the kitchen. "Are you home?" he called out again.

"Must not be," he said under his breath, looking at Kim, and showing a disappointed look on his face. "He may have gone to church, and hasn't made it back yet." he said, squeezing her hand and pulling out a chair. "Sometimes he stops at the convenience store in town and sometimes he goes to a friend's house after church. Sit here and I'll go see if he's in the living room, or maybe he's still in bed. He did come in rather late last night."

Robert went off down the hall, and then disappeared into a room. Kim sat down at the table, and watched as he came out of one room, looked at her, raised his hands in doubt, then disappeared into another. She sat there, watching, waiting, wondering what she would say to the

father of the man she knew she wanted to be with for the rest of her life when he came out and stood before her for the very first time.

What if he didn't like her? What if she didn't like him? What would they do? Break up and never see each other again?

"No. We were meant to be together, and we will be together. He will like me, and I will like him, I just know it!" she thought to herself.

Robert came back, looked at her, spread his arms out wide, and sat down at the table. "I found this piece of paper stuck to the refrigerator door," Kim said reaching out and handing it to him. He took it, looked at it, and then started reading it aloud.

"It's a note from Dad. He's gone to do a head, and should be back in a couple of hours. 'Your dinner's in the fridge. Watch TV, or take a nap.' At the bottom he says, 'I'm glad you went to church with your girlfriend. Then he says, "Bring her to the house sometimes."

"Oh Robert," she said looking up at him and smiling. I just know your father's a great person. I love him already! But what does he mean? Gone to do a head? What kind of language is that?"

"That," Robert said, raising his shoulder and smiling, "is what he tells me when well, when he has a head to do! He's a hair stylist. He styles and cuts women's hair and he's very popular.

Women call him at all hours wanting him to fix their hair. Usually they make an appointment and go to his salon down town. But sometimes a party or a wedding or some emergency comes up, where they need someone's hair done in a hurry, and they don't have time to go down town to his salon. When that happens they call him here, and he goes to their homes, and fixes their hair. He must be very good at it, because they keep calling him, and they pay extra for it. If I'm here when he leaves, he tells me where he's going. If I'm not, he leaves a note telling me, he's gone to someone's house to do a head. One day as I was driving in, he was driving out, and he was obviously in a big hurry because he didn't leave me a note that day, and as we passed each other. He rolled the glass down in his car, and began to holler out that he was going to do a head of hair. Later when I asked him the same question you just asked me. He told me when he left the house, he was driving so fast, that when he saw me coming., he only had time to say he was going to do a head before a bug bounced off his hand, spattered all over his face. He had to close his mouth, and roll the glass back up. He said that bug was so big that he had to use his customer's bathroom to wash his face and hands before he could style her hair."

Robert sat up straight in the chair, ran his open hand across his face, looked at Kim, then leaned forward, and started rocking his body back and forth. "I don't know why he shortened what he needed to tell me each time before he left," he said. "I guess it was because he was in a hurry to leave, each time he told me! After repeating his abbreviated version of where he was going to me over and over for the past several days, before he went out on a house call, I think he figured I understood where he was going, and never bothered to replace the two missing words. But it's not a part of any language. It's just a phrase he uses to let me know he's going out to do a head of hair."

Robert got up from the table, walked to the sink, wadded the note up and threw it in the trash can. "It's an old note. I forgot to throw away anyway," he said. "Want me to make some coffee?" he said looking at her and smiling.

"No," she answered. "I don't drink it, but I will take a coke."

He got two Cokes from the refrigerator and then walked back and sat down at the table.   "Come sit here in my lap," he said patting his legs with his hands. "I want to ask you a question."

She got up slowly, pushed her chair back against the table, and stood there looking at him.

"Is it safe?" she said turning and starting to move towards him. I don't want your dad to walk in and see me sitting in your lap. Not that we would be doing anything bad, but us being alone and all, he might think I was trying to take advantage of you.

"You want me to get out of your lap?"

"No," he said kissing her on the cheek. "I want you to stay right where you're at and if my dad comes in and wonders what we're doing, I'll tell him I told you to sit on my lap and take advantage of me."

She laughed and put both her arms back around his neck. "You'll do no such thing," she said as she pulled him towards her and let his head rest against her breast. But you better let me know when he gets here, so I can get out of your lap before he comes in, or he might think we're both bad!"

"Don't worry," he said moving his lips down her neck. "There is nothing he dislikes more, than to come home and find my truck in his parking place and then he has to wait for me to come outside and move it before he can park his car and go inside the house. Trust me, I've done this before. He'll keep blowing his horn, until I go out there and move my truck."

She pulled her arms from around his neck, and pushed him away. "You've done this before with other girls, haven't you?"

"No," he said kissing her neck again. "I've done it before, but for other reasons."

"What other reasons could there be?" she asked. "You better tell me the truth."

"Well," he said lifting his heels off the floor to reposition her body on his lap, "he's always getting phone calls from different women, wanting him to come to their house, and fix their hair. "He tells me to answer them, get their number, and tell them he will call them back. 'But don't tell them to call the office,' he says. He says they're too busy there to schedule house calls. I answer them and tell them he's not at home. They tell me it's important that they speak to him. I take their number, and tell them he will call them back as soon as he comes in. I'm usually tired and give out when I come in from school, and I'm afraid I'll fall asleep before he gets here, or I'll forget to tell him they called so I try to remind myself that I'm supposed to tell him something. I leave my truck in his parking place, so he will blow his horn when he comes in, and I'll have to go out and move it, and I'll remember and give him the messages. And sometimes, I just leave my truck in his space, because I miss him and want to see him."

She put her arms back around his neck. "Aren't you the smart one," she said as she kissed him and then rested her head against his chest. She pulled herself up in his lap, winked and smiled at him, then wet her little finger, and slowly and deliberately pushed it in and out of her mouth.

"Now what was that question you wanted to ask me?" she said smiling and looking up at him. "And if it is 'Can I spend the night with you?' the answer is no. You promised my mama, you'd have me home for dinner tonight, and once I get there, she won't let me go out again."

She kissed her little finger, and then placed it on his lips. That should teach you to be careful what you promise."

"That's not fair," he said reaching both his arms under her legs, and standing up quickly and walking off toward the bedroom with her in his arms. "You're supposed to let me ask you the question before you give me the answer."

He stopped and stood there for a moment, facing the bedroom, then turned and carried her back to the table and gingerly sat her down in the nearest chair.

"I did say you would have the finally say in such matters, didn't I?" He looked admiringly at her and sat down in a chair on the other side of the table. "But there is a question I have to ask you, and it is a serious one. He sat there looking at her from across the table. "Gosh, she is so beautiful," he thought. "I am so lucky to have met her. I don't know how I've lived this long, without knowing her. If I'd met her later, and she would have been married to someone else, I'd just died!" He folded his palms together, and looked straight into her eyes. "I would never take advantage of you, or do anything to hurt you." he said. "You know that, don't you? I love you so much, and I would never lie to you. I'm sitting here right now starting at you, telling myself that whoever marries you, will be the luckiest man alive, and his children will have the best mother in the whole world. I'm telling you now, in front of God and everybody, that I want to be that man, and I want to be the father of those wonderful children! I had hoped, before we started back to your place, the rain would stop, and the sun would come out, drying the road a little, and making it safe to drive on. But it looks like that's not going to happen! It's rained even harder since we've been here, and even if we started back now, I'm afraid that road out there will be so muddy and slippery, that no vehicle will be able to stay on it. I know you wanted to meet my dad, and I wanted you to meet him too, but if he doesn't get here soon, I don't think either one of us will meet him tonight."

He reached out and took her hand, and put it in between the two of his. "You know how slippery and muddy the road was when we came in on it? It's even more dangerous to travel on now, and unless he is already on it. I don't think he will get near that road until it dries up some.

He's already slid off of it three times, and the last time it happened, he had to walk home. You should have been here and seen him. He was covered all over with mud! It took nearly a day and a half for the road to dry enough so the wrecker could get in and pull his car out of the ditch."

The expression on her face changed as the sound of loud music from an old song she liked, but had forgotten had caught her ear. She pulled her arm back, and turned her head towards the sound, and listened attentively to the popular ring tone on the cell phone. He folded his hands together, got up and walked to the side of the table, picked up the phone, turned and looked back at her. "This may be dad, I'd better answer it. Hello? Yes. How is the road? Glad you got through. No, don't blow your horn. I'm coming right out."

And then she heard him say, "You have a visitor." Robert pushed the two ends of the cell phone together, ending the call and then put the phone back down on the table. "That was Dad," he said. He's in the driveway now, waiting for me to go move my truck so he can park his car and come inside the house."

CHAPTER 14

In his many stops over at Samuel's Convenient Store and Restaurant, Matt had never spent so much time driving around the parking lot looking for a place to park except for once. When the city in conjunction with the Grand Opening of the new Restaurant brought in the coach and each member of the High School Girls Basketball Team to celebrate they're winning the state championship. The owner of the building gave away free hamburgers and soft drinks to promote the opening of his new Restaurant. Matt remembered the event. It wasn't too long ago he thought, as he continued to look for a place to park his car. I think the whole town must have come out that night! I know all the teachers and most of the high school students did, he recalled. He remembered the owner's wife telling him one day while he fixed her hair. That her husband complained all the time about spending a small fortune on those hamburgers and soft drinks he gave away, what a celebration that was, he said to himself.

I don't think what's going on here today could possibly top the appreciation and approval the town's people paid the girls and the coach that night. Still, he couldn't help but wonder what could be happening inside, that so many people had come out to see. He really didn't care though, his curiosity wasn't bothering him one bit. He would have given up looking for a parking place long ago, when he first turned off the highway, and saw the parking lot was full.

But he needed to stop and buy a couple of items from the store, and after holding his temper in tact for the last few minutes. He could use a cup of that strong black coffee from the restaurant.

Almost ever Sunday afternoon on his way home from church, for the past several months. Matt had made a habit of turning off the highway, and driving into the parking lot at the Convenient Store, and going inside, and buying two lottery tickets. Then having a cup of coffee in the Restaurant before driving home. But today as he drove around the building for the second time, wondering why the parking lot was so crowded he noticed the surrounding area parking lots were just as crowded. Must be the weather he decided, looking at all the parked cars.

Its rained so much for so long, everybody in town must have come here to do the same thing he was about to do.

When a small truck, a short distance in front of him started backing out freeing a parking space Matt stopped his car. He turned his signal light on, indicating to any oncoming driver that as soon as the truck backed out, he was planning to park his car in the empty space. Then backed his car up just enough for the truck to back out, and get in front of him and leave. The driver of the truck didn't leave right away though. He took his time backing out, took even more time moving his vehicle out of Matt's way. Exposing the empty parking space to any oncoming vehicle looking for a place to park jeopardizing Matt's chances of getting it. As soon as the truck did back out, and start to move forward, another car started coming toward him. Fearing the other car would get the parking space Matt sped up, and turned into the vacant space at the very same time the oncoming car did, causing both drivers to slam down hard on their brakes to avoid hitting each other head on.

Both cars came to a sudden stop; their front ends almost touching the other, stuck halfway inside the one parking space. Neither car could move forward without hitting the other, nor neither driver volunteered to back his car out, and let the other car in. They both just sat there, staring at each other, creating a stalemate. Matt thought about getting out and telling the other driver in no certain language. That this was his parking place, he found it first, and he had no intentions of letting someone who had just pulled in off the highway have it. He put his engine in park, put his hand on the door handle, hesitated a moment, then looked up, and continued staring at the other driver. What am I doing, he asked himself, after a few minutes of trying to stare the other driver down. This is ridiculous; it's not worth ruining my day over. I'll find another parking place, if I don't, I'll go home. He hesitated another moment, then moved his hand off the door handle, took the engine out of park, put it in reverse and slowly backed out.

CHAPTER 15

The rain had stopped, as Matt made another circle around the building, then slowed down, and spotted a couple in front of him, standing beside the open doors of their parked vehicle.

As he drew closer, he couldn't be sure whether the couple had just arrived, and were getting out of their vehicle or whether they were getting into their vehicle, and preparing to leave, but he couldn't pass this opportune up. If they were leaving, he had to have that parking place! He stopped his car, turned his signal light on, and was thinking about backing up, when he saw the couple get inside their vehicle, close the doors, and begin to back out. He started to back up himself, when he noticed the back signal light from the other vehicle come on. Indicating the driver in the parking space was backing out, and would be leaving in the same direction that he had just came from. Limiting the chances of any oncoming vehicle getting the parking space, before he did. He took a handkerchief from his pocket, whipped it across his face, and breathed a sigh of relief.

This was the same thing he drove away from only a few minutes ago, and now it was happening again. But this time there was one big difference! The vehicle backing out was backing into the road, preventing any other vehicle coming up behind it from passing. There was no vehicle coming at the moment he noticed, but if there had been that driver would have to stop and wait, for the vehicle in front of him to leave, giving him the big advantage.

Matt put the handkerchief back in his pocket, and smiled to himself. No need to back up now he said, feeling content that he would have no trouble claiming his parking space. I'm glad I drove away, and let that other driver have my last parking place, he said to himself. This is a much better spot anyway, right in front of the entrance, don't have to walk so far to get inside, and that comes in handy in this wet unpleasant weather.

It had been raining off and on for the past two days, sometimes at a hard pace, but for the most part, the rain fell in a slow steady drizzle. At the moment the sky was clear, the clouds had disappeared, and the sun was trying to break through. Matt pulled his car into the newly found parking space, and stepped out on the damp pavement. Water was standing in small puddles in several low spots across the parking lot, where the pavement had sunk in, and in other places where the lot was not paved; the ground was wet and soggier. He locked the doors to his car, and started walking toward the front door of the building.

It was his intent to get in, get what he needed, and get right out. Then get started for home before it started raining again. He was hoping out in the county where he lived, the rain had stopped completely, and the sun had dried up the wet muddy dirt road that he had to drive home on tonight. He reached the front steps, then turned and saw a woman walking hurriedly from another direction toward him. He stooped down on the step to tie his shoelace, waited for the woman to catch up with him, and rose up, and smiled at her. Then held the front door open, and let her walk in before him. Now why did I do that, he asked himself, as he watched the woman walk towards the cashier counter and fumble in her purse. I wasn't just being polite. My shoelaces weren't untied; I just pretended they were, so she could catch up with me. I wanted to see what she looked like! Matt let go of the door, and followed her into the store.

He took two one dollars bills from his wallet to purchase two lottery tickets, and walked up to the cashier's counter, and stood waiting in line behind the woman he'd just let walk in before him. She was pretty, and she smelled so good, he admitted to himself, as he heard her tell the clerk she wanted four lottery tickets. Then as she walked away, he took the two tickets, he'd ordered, and put them in his pocket, turned and started walking away. Then stopped a little ways from the counter, and picked up something from off the floor. He put the newly found object in his pocket, then started looking around for the woman that had bought tickets in front of him. He'd seen her twice today for the first time in his life, and then only for a moment or two before she came into the store. But those two brief moments were enough to let him know that he wanted to see her again. He didn't know what it was, but when he stood behind her, there was something about that woman that made him feel good inside. Like he was a teenager again, and for the second time in his life, he was in love!

He'd been around women all his life, beautiful women, he worked with them but not since his wife died, had he ever felt attracted to any of them, like he did to this woman. It was like she was wearing a magnet drawing him to her! He spotted her standing over near the restaurant, and started walking towards her. What if she won't talk to me, what if she turns and walks away, when she sees me coming, he heard himself thinking. I'm acting like a teenager already, he told himself, there's no reason for her not to talk to me. Besides, I have something that belongs to her, and she'll want me to give it back.

"Excuse me lady," he almost shouted, as he approached her. "I was standing next in line behind you waiting to buy tickets myself, and I saw you pay that clerk for four lottery tickets. I wasn't trying to be nosey, but when you stepped out and turned around to leave. I noticed you put only three tickets in your purse. I don't know what happen to the fourth one; maybe you kept it out for a special reason. I didn't think anymore about it until I walked upon you now, and I must tell you. I'd feel very bad about myself. If I let you leave this building, without telling you, that I saw you put in your purse, three lottery tickets, when I know you purchased four. Especially if that fourth ticket turned out to be the winning one, and I let you walk out of here believing you had it in your purse! It's really none of my business, but I'd hate to know the winning ticket, was the one you didn't put in your purse.

She turned and looked at him like she was about to call the law, then quickly opened her purse, and ran to an empty booth, and dumped the contents out on the table, and seen the three lottery tickets. "Your right, there's only three here," she said, holding them up to show him.

"That clerk kept one of my lottery tickets!" She put everything back in her purse, except the three tickets. "Wait here will you please," she said turning and starting to go back to the counter.

"I'm going to talk to that clerk, and you may have to help me make him give me back the other one."

"No he shouted, moving forward and, reaching out to stop her, he doesn't have the other one. I have it!" She turned and faced him.

"You have it," she said looking like maybe she should have called the law. "How did you get it?"

"I found it on the floor, shortly after I purchased mine," he said. "You must have dropped it, when you put the other three in your purse."

She sat down at the table and lowered her head. "And I was about to accuse that clerk of keeping one of my tickets. You must think I'm a terrible person. Why would you even want to give it back?"

"Well," he said looking at her, and trying not to look too anxious. "I was hopping you'd do something for me."

"Yes," she said, looking up at him, and smiling. "By all means, what can I do for you?"

He sat down at the booth across the table from her. "Let me buy you a cup of coffee."

CHAPTER 16

"**D**o you drink a lot of coffee," she asked, after they both were seated, and the waiter brought two steaming cups of black coffee to their table?

"My son says I do," he answered. She looked him and smiled.

"I drink some in the mornings and some in the afternoons myself, and my daughter says the same thing about me. Why is it when we parents like to drink coffee, our children can hardly stand the taste of it. Yet its usually the other way around, when we don't like it, they tend to love it! My teenage daughter drinks a half of a cup in the mornings, with her grandfather and me, but I think she does it, just to please me."

"You have a daughter," he said looking at her, with his mouth wide open!"

"Yes I do, and she just graduated from high school."

"No," he said dragging the word out, then closing his mouth. You're too young to have a daughter graduating from high school. You look like you just finished a couple of years ago yourself."

"Thank you, she said, you're very kind but I do have a daughter that just graduated from high school, and I am old enough, and if your trying to score points with me, your succeeding!" They both laughed, and he leaned back, and picked up his coffee cup.

"Well, in that case then, I hope she looks exactly like her mother."

She raised herself up on the seat, and leaned forward. "Why, she said looking directly into his eyes, would you say anything like that? I always thought she looked like her dad."

He sat his cup back down on the table, and reached out and touched her hand. "What I meant was, if she looks exactly like you I know you got to have a very beautiful daughter."

"Oh your not only kind, but your sweet too," she said. "If I don't win the lottery, I hope you win it!" They both looked at each other, and then started laughing. "But I am concerned," she said. "She was supposed to practice in a church play today but they canceled it for some reason. One of the players got sick, and they couldn't replace him, I think. She left right after church and went to the movies with a boy she met only yesterday, and like every mother, I'm worried about her."

He called the waiter, and ordered two more coffees, and two slices of apple pie. "I wouldn't worry too much, he said, reaching out, and touching her hand again. If she met him at church, he's probably a good boy."

"She didn't meet him at church, she said, that's the amazing part. He came here and picked her up, and took her to church! It's a long complicated story." She waved her hand in front of his face. "I'm boring you; you probably don't want to hear all this."

He caught her hand in mid air. "Yes I do he said, and your certainly not boring me. I'm very much interest in hearing about you and your daughter."

"Well ok then", she said taking a piece of her pie, then looking up at him. "That boy out there with my daughter right now, came to the house yesterday to talk to Papa, that's my daughter's grandfather, we call him Papa. I didn't know him, but he told my ten year old son who went to the door, that he was here on a school project. Something about talking to an old person, and writing a report, could get him the extra credit he needed to graduate from high school. So I told my son to let him in. She picked up her cup and swallowed some coffee, then set it back down on the table, and shook her head. "That coffee's hot, just the way I like it. Well to make a long story short, like I said before, he came here to talk to Papa, but Papa had gone back to bed, and wouldn't talk to him. So I left him sitting on the couch in the living room, thinking I'd sent my son to get Papa up. But Papa wouldn't get up, and I got busy doing something else, and I hate to admit it, but I forgot all about him. But I have to tell you when I did talk to him later; I found that he was a very intelligent young man, and good looking too! Well, when my daughter came home about an hour later, I told her there was a boy sitting on the couch, out there in the room all by himself, waiting to talk to Papa. But Papa had laid down, and wouldn't get back up, and I asked her to go in there, and bring him something cold to drink, and tell him to come back tomorrow, which she did." She smiled and repositioned herself in the booth.

You want me to go on?" He nodded his head that he did. "They didn't know each other when she went into that room. But when my son and I got him off the floor, and my daughter got on the couch with him, and they walked out of that room together, it was like they'd known each other for all their lives. My daughter had fallen over him, into him, and for him, and he had caught her, held her, and met her, all at the same time. They both benefited from something that happened in the room that caused them to have an accident, through no fault of their own, even though they caused it themselves. I like to think that some divine intervention took place," she said. "But whatever it was, I know that after it was over, and we all sat down on the couch together. I was so overcome with the joy I saw on both of their faces, that I felt obliged to introduce him to the rest of my family."

She put a small piece of pie in her mouth, and swallowed a sip of her coffee. "That happened yesterday she said, and I'm here today, because of it! My daughter invited him to eat dinner with us tonight, and I had to come here to find some extra things to fix."

He reached out and took her hand, and this time she let him hold it for a second or two, then she pulled it back, and looked at him and smiled. "Then I have your daughter to thank for sending you here," he said smiling back at her. "Thank her for me, will you. I'll thank her myself if I ever get to see her, and I guess that boy played a part in sending you here too. Looks like I owe them both a big thank you he said, smiling, and it sounds like your daughter and that boy are off to a great start."

"Thanks she said, I'll tell her you said that. I know she'll be happy to here that a stranger I met in town today, said for me to be sure and tell her that he was interested in hearing about you." She laughed and reached out and took his hand. "I truly hope this is the right boy for her, its really the first one she's been out with." She squeezed his hand and pulled it toward her. "Seriously, I'm really glad I came, and I'm glad we met. When I dropped that lottery ticket on the floor, it was an accident. But when you found it, and gave it back to me, and we sat down at that table, it was like a miracle had just happened. Not that I got the ticket back, but that I got the feeling back, I'd lost years ago, when my husband died."

He wanted to get up and move across the table, and take her in his arms, and shower her with kisses, and tell her what a blessing, meeting her here was to him. But instead, he just sat there, and looked at her from across the table and realized how lonely he'd been all these years since his wife had died, and how beautiful this woman sitting in front of him was. "Tell me more about your daughter and that boy he said, looking straight into her eyes, and how you think divine purpose caused those accidents that brought them together."

"Well she said reaching out for his hand; I don't know which one it was that sealed the bond between them. The accident when Kim fell over him, or the accident when Papa hit Robert on the back of the head, either one of them, or both I think was meant to happen."

"Wait a minute," he said, letting go of her hand, and jumping up and looking at her.

"What did you say the boy's name was?"

"Robert, she said, noticing the change of color on his face, why? My son's name is Robert, he said leaning over the table. You don't think, no it couldn't be," he said. "What did you say your daughter's name was?"

"I didn't" she said, leaning forward, and reaching out again for his hand.

"My son did say he had a new girlfriend" he said, as he sat back down. I think she's his first really. At least she is the first one he's told me about, but he didn't mention her name. He was taking her to the movies today. I told him they could go to the movies any day, during the week, but on a Sunday, he should take her to church. Later before he left the house, he told me she called, and said there'd been a change of plans, and asked him if he would take her to church?"

"Kim, that's my daughter's name, and she did call him, and he did come to the house, and they did leave going to church together," she said, looking at him, and beginning to show some signs of nervousness.

"Did you see him," he asked?

"Yes of course I saw him she said, and he was a very charming boy."

"Did he say anything about his family." he asked squeezing her hand, and wondering whether he should look more concerned.

"No she said, he only spoke of going to church a lot with his mother, when she was alive."

"His mother did take him with her most of the time, before she died," he said. "Did Robert ever say anything about where he lived," he asked.

"No she said shaking her head, although once he did say he'd better leave and get back home, while he still could. I wondered what he meant by that, but I didn't ask.

"Was it raining that day?" he asked, raising up off his seat, and leaning over the table towards her.

"Yes I believe it was," she said, rising up off her seat, and leaning forward herself.

"That explains it then." he said, jumping up and throwing his arms out over the table, and pulling her to him. Your daughter and my son are dating each other!"

They stood there, two bodies, male and female, leaning across the table from each other, both brought together simultaneous by an outburst of a shared interest in one common cause. Their arms wrapped around the other, their lips sealed together for one silent moment, and then they heard the clapping of hands, and sat back down. "Do you know what just happened?" she asked, glancing around at the people, and then looking back at him.

"Yes he said, reaching for her hand, and smiling. We just kissed each other, and the crowd applauded!"

"No," she said, looking into his eyes, and squeezing his hand. "Two strangers that didn't even know each other's names just met!"

He smiled stood up, and offered his hand for her to shake. "My name is Matt Lambert," he said, and I'm mighty glad to make your acquaintance. She rose up reached out, and shook his hand. "I'm glad to meet you too she said, and my name is Katie Powel, and I'd love to stay and get acquainted with you but whether that's your son out there with my daughter or not. He's supposed to have her back here for dinner tonight, and I asked him to stay and eat with us. Well Kim did, but I agreed to it, and I image their both going to be pretty hungry when they get here."

They both sat back down, and stared across the table at each other. "I don't want my future-son-in-law to think his future mother-in-law is a bad cook," she said, breaking the silent. "So I guess I'd better get on home, and start looking for something good to cook. Why don't you come and eat with us too." she said. "Give us both a chance to get to know each other better."

"Well," he said reaching out and holding her hand. "There is nothing I'd like more, and a home cooked meal prepared by such a beautiful woman, sounds mighty tempting. But tonight, I think we better let our kids get the chance to know each other better. Why don't you give me your phone number, and let me call you tomorrow?"

"Ok" she said, writing her number down on a piece of paper, and scribbling. "Call me early on it."

He took the paper, looked at it, put it in his pocket, smiled and put four one dollar bills on a saucer. Then walked to the other side of the table, put his arms around her, kissed her lightly on the cheek, picked up the check, and left the building.

CHAPTER 17

Matt stopped the car in front of his house, put the engine in park, and waited for his son to come and move his truck out of his parking place. He watched as Robert came out of the house, jumped into his truck, revved the engine up a couple of times to let him know he was there, then started backing out. I wonder why he still parks his truck in my place, Matt thought while he was waiting, when he knows he'll have to come out and move it when I came in. He thought about asking him several times before, but figured he had his reasons, and never did.

Matt watched him park his truck, then turned his head and leaned back against the seat. That boy is a grown man now, he thought to himself. He'll be getting married soon, and moving out and this old house will be a lonely place to live in. He never thought of being lonely before, he never had to! Even after his wife died, he wasn't really lonely, he had Robert. They were always together; he even went to work with him at times. But now with Robert gone, and him living in this house by himself, he would be lonely for the first time, and he wasn't sure he could handle it. He thought of Katie, and what it would be like to have her move in with him, and the thought he'd been entertaining all evening in the back of his mind of replacing his son's departure with Katie's arrival, began to sound more and more like it wasn't such a bad idea after all.

His son was dating Katie's daughter, he had no doubt about that, and he was dating Katie's daughter's mother, or at least he thought he might soon be! Wouldn't it be something?

If my son ended up marring my girl friend's daughter and my son's wife's mother ended up marring me. His daughter's husband's father! That would be something, he thought.

Matt pulled himself up in the seat, saw the unoccupied space in front of him, put the engine in drive and slowly pulled his car into the empty parking place. Driving on that dirt road is always a tiring chore, he thought as he killed the engine, and stepped out onto the garage floor.

But driving on it, when it was wet and muddy, with the thought of getting stuck in the mud or sliding off the road, dancing around in the back of your mind made it a grueling punishing experience. He would have stayed in town tonight, and gone to work the next day, straight from his hotel, since he had an extra suit of clothes in his car. Or he could have stayed in the room he had in the back of his office. But he enjoyed going home each day and spending time with his son, and Robert seemed to enjoy being there with him. And two, he wanted to see him, and find out how things went with him and his new girlfriend today.

He opened the door, and stepped into the house. I wonder who the visitor is, Robert mentioned. Maybe someone's here to tell me I've won the lottery. He closed the door, and started walking towards the kitchen, where Robert usually sat waiting at the table to drink a cup of fresh coffee with him. But as he drew near, he saw Robert in the hallway, and instead of holding a cup of hot coffee in his hand and sitting at the table. He was standing in the doorway, holding the hand of a beautiful tall young attractive red headed girl.

Matt continued walking towards them, this must be my visitor, Katie's daughter, he thought.

She is lovely just like her mother, he said to himself, as he moved up and stood in front of her.

"And who is this pretty little lady, he asked looking directly at her and, reaching his open hand out? Then quickly turning his head, and looking at Robert, "and how did you get back in the house so quick? Although I can see why you would want to he said, looking back at the girl.

He continued looking at her, and then glanced back at his son. "I didn't know you went to another state this morning, when you left the house. He said, as he looked back at the girl, and moved a little closer to her. "But you must have he said, looking straight into her eyes because we don't have any females in this state, half as beautiful as she is!"

"Thank you," she whispered, turning her head, and looking at Robert.

"Dad," Robert said, moving closer to Kim, and putting his arms around her. "I want you to meet my girlfriend, Kim. And Kim," he said smiling and looking at her, then waving his hand toward his dad. This is Matt, my dad. We went to church together, he said, putting his arms back around Kim and pulling her close to him. We were going to the movies, but she insisted on coming out here instead." He pulled her closer to her, and looked at his dad. She wanted to meet you!"

Matt looked at them both, and then reached his hand out to Robert. "Welcome son, I'm glad you brought her. She is most welcome here, both of you are," he said shaking Robert's hand, then turning back and facing the girl. "You won't mind if I give you a big welcome home hug will you, instead of a hand shake," he said smiling and reaching his arms out towards her.

"Robert squeezed my hand a little too hard, and it's still hurting!"

CHAPTER 18

"**D**ad Robert said, there's something I need to talk to you about. Can it wait son, I'm telling your girlfriend what beautiful long silky hair she has, and how much I'd like to style it. I could fix it this evening, if you two aren't going someplace, he said, as he led her to the couch and sat down beside her. "It'll only take about an hour and I guarantee you'll like it." He looked at Robert, and then moved a little closer to her. "Robert didn't tell you didn't he?" he said, smiling at her. "That's how I make my living, cutting and styling women's hair."

She looked at Robert, "Yes he told me she said looking back at him, and he said you were very good at it. My mother and I will probably be making an appointment with you very soon."

"You won't have to do that my dear," he said. "In fact I will be very hurt, if you do."

"All you or your mother will have to do is walk in, or call me, and you will be taken care of right away."

Robert came back from the kitchen, and sat down on the couch beside his dad. "It's still raining, slow, but still raining," he said looking at Kim, and trying to smile.

Matt turned and looked at his son. "You and your girlfriend may as well settle in, and plan on staying here for awhile," he said, looking at them both. "Because right now, that road out there is in no condition for anyone to be driving on, and even if it stopped raining altogether, and the sun came out. I'd still advise against going anywhere for the next two or three hours, and not even then unless things outside dries up a lot. I made it home only because the weather changed briefly in my favor, and I was fortunate enough to take advance of it." He turned and looked back at Kim. "And you pretty little lady," he said smiling, and looking straight into her eyes."

"I strongly advise you to call your mother, and tell her you won't be able to make it home for dinner tonight. Tell her you came here with Robert to meet me, and that I'm here with you now. She may want to talk to me, if she does, let me talk to her, and don't worry, we're going to get you home, just as soon as that road dries up a little. And while your waiting, think about letting me fix your hair. I got some magazines you can look at, and maybe you'll see a style you'll like."

He leaned back, and looked at Robert. "You said you wanted to talk to me, so let's go over there and sit at the table he said getting up from the couch, while your girlfriend calls her mother, we can talk."

"Dad," Robert said as he sat down across the table from him. I promised Kim's mother, I'd have her daughter home by six o'clock tonight. She's planning a big dinner for us, and she trusts me to have her there. If I don't show up, she'll never trust me again." He threw his arms up in the air, and looked at his dad. "But what can I do, there's no way I can take her home tonight! That road is the only way out of here, and is so wet and muddy right now, that my truck wouldn't stay on it for one block, much less two miles. Even if I got on it and tried to take her home, I'd

get stuck in the mud, or slide off in the ditch before I got started."
He stood up, and looked towards the hallway for Kim, who was
still on the phone talking to her mother, and then sat back down
at the table. Even if it stops raining, and the sun does start
shining," he said. "It's going to be tomorrow afternoon, if not
later before that road dries up enough for any vehicle to get on it."

He ran his open fingers through his hair, then put both his
hands on the table, and looked at his dad. "And how am I going
to convince her, that I didn't just let her come out here on
purpose? She's going to think I knew full well, I wouldn't be able
to get back on that road, and drive her home tonight.

"Oh I don't think she will be thinking anything like that," Matt
said, looking back at his son and smiling. "Didn't you tell me she
insisted on coming out here? Yes she wanted to meet you, and I
swear, I had every intendances of leaving, right after you got here.
But while we were waiting, she wanted to look at all the pictures
we had, and I think I told her the story behind each one of them,"
he said smiling. The rain had stopped some, but not completely,
and I swear to you again, that with her excitement over the
pictures, and my memories of them I just forgot about the
urgency for us to leave."

"You don't have to swear to me son, I believe you, and your
girlfriend will to, and if her mother doubts it. We'll just have to
convince her to come over to our side."

Kim came back into the room, and sat down at the table beside
Robert. She looked up at him and smiled. "She wants to talk to
your father."

Matt looked at her winked, and then took the cell phone.
"Thank you, I'll be right back," he said as he left the room.

"So, that really was your son out there with my daughter,"
Katie said, after Matt said hello into the phone. And he's not

going to have my daughter back here by six o'clock tonight like he promised, is he?"

"No, Matt answered, but let me tell you why?"

"I already know why," Katie answered. "He waited too long before deciding to start back. Leaving my little girl with no choice, but to stay, and spend the night with him! But she covered for him, she blamed herself. Robert wanted them to leave early while they could, before the road got in too bad a shape to drive on, but she wanted to stay and meet you. She told me about it. Doesn't that make you feel good Mr. Lambert, to know that both mother and daughter wanted to meet you? I've heard those stories of people sliding off into the ditch, road washing out, and people leaving their vehicle stuck in the mud, and having to walk home. Makes you feel a little sorry for those folks living in the county, who travel back and fourth into town, like yourself," she said. I had a friend once that lived on one of those unpaved roads and she wouldn't even leave home when it rained. So I believe my daughter, Robert can't bring her home tonight. I'm not blaming anyone, and I certainly don't want him trying to bring her home, until that road is safe enough to travel on. I'm hoping it dries up enough so both of you can bring her home soon, and help me eat some of this food that was left, when the couple in question didn't show up."

She moved the cell phone from her ear, stretched her arm out, cleared her throat, then brought her arm back to her ear, and continued talking. "You haven't told them that we know each other yet, have you," she asked?"

"No," he answered, noticing the higher pitch in her voice.

"Well don't," she said. "Cause if my little girl doesn't come home, the same way she was when she left home. We won't!"

"We won't what," he asked?

"We won't know each other," she answered. "My daughter may have to spend the night with your son, but she doesn't have to go to bed with him"

"Of course she doesn't, and she won't," he answered. He lowered his voice, and almost whispered into the phone. "You don't have to concern yourself about that, it won't happen!"

"My son told me, they both signed one of those pledges in school to abstain from having sex until after marriage, and I'll be right here with them to make sure they honor it.

"Well you just remember what I'm telling you right here and now," she said putting her lips against the phone, and whispering softly into it. "If you have any visions at all of ever sleeping in my bed," she paused a second to let him grasp the meaning of what she was saying. "You will make certain that it doesn't happen!"

"My daughter was a virgin when she left here, and if you want those visions of yours

to become a reality." She paused again, and then continued, her voice changing to a soft gentle sound. "You'll see that she comes back here a virgin!" Now let me say a few words to Robert please."

Matt gave the cell phone to Robert, and went back into the kitchen where Kim sat waiting at the table.

"Everything's alright," he said as he pulled out a chair, and sat down across the table from her. "Your mother just wants to tell Robert to take good care of her pretty little girl, he said, smiling at her, she told me the same thing, and that's exactly what we're going to do."

CHAPTER 19

Matt rolled the stool Kim was sitting on around, so she could look at herself in the dressing room mirror, and see what he had done to her hair. "You like it," he signaled to her through the glass, as he put his comb and brush down, and stood looking at her face in the mirror from behind the stool?

"Oh Mr. Lambert," Kim said feeling her hair, and smiling back at him. "You are the best, I've never seen my hair looking so good! I can't wait to get home and show it to everyone."

He put his hand on her shoulder to keep the stool in place, and looked at her face in the mirror. "Hold it right there pretty little lady. My son tells me he asked you to marry him, and you said yes. I am pleased that you accepted, and it makes me happy to know that I will become both your hairdresser and your father-in-law. But I got to tell you right here and now, there is one thing I will expect my future daughter-in-law to do."

She took her hands down from her hair, put her foot on the floor, and shoved the stool around until she was facing him. "And what will that be Mr. Lambert?"

He took a step backward looked into her face, and smiled. "Just that she forgets all that Mr. Lambert stuff, and calls me Matt!" She got up from the stool, and walked over, and stood beside the bed. "Is this where Robert sleeps," she asked, sitting down on the edge.

"No he said, his room, and my room is at the other end of the hall. This is the guest room, it's where you will sleep, if we can't get you home tonight. Of course, I'll vacuum the floor, and tidy the place up a bit." he said.

"You don't have to do that she said, your giving me a free hair do, show me where the vacuum cleaner is, and let me do it."

"Thanks he said smiling at her, but I'm used to it. I give Robert and his friends haircuts in here, sometimes, and believe me, after I'm finished, the whole floor needs vacuuming."

She got up from the edge of the bed, and stood in front of the mirror. "This is a nice room Matt, I like it, and I like the way you fixed my hair. I can just hear mother when she sees it. Who fixed your hair, she'll say? Its beautiful, whoever it was, has got to fix mine the very same way."

He smiled, and said thanks. "You tell your mother, I'll fix her hair anytime, any way she wants it."

She turned around, and looked right at him. "Can I see Robert's room?"

"Sure, he said, I'll go get him to show it to you."

She reached out and touched his arm. "I want you to show it to me."

"Ok he said, but wouldn't you rather see it with Robert?"

"No she said, I want the bed we both see together, to be the bed we share together."

He turned and started walking toward the door. "Come on then, I'll show it to you. There's an extra blanket in the closet if you need it tonight, he said as they walked out the door.

The next morning came too soon for Matt. Too much of his sleep time was wasted staying awake listening for sounds, any sound that would alert him to what he hoped would not happened. Right after Kim left them last night, and went back to her room, to go to bed, he remembered staying at the kitchen table and discussing some of the day's events with his son.

At that time he let it be known that the guest room was off limits to him for as long as Kim was staying in it, and he made it clear that the off limits meant during the day, as well as the night.

He explained the reasons, and even told him that Kim said she wanted it that way. They had stayed up and talked for a short while, before going to bed themselves, and Matt had no doubt that his son would go straight to his room and go right to sleep. In fact he felt confident that he didn't need to say anything more about the need for him to stay out of the guest room. He didn't feel too good about keeping them apart; after all they were in love. But they would be married soon he thought, so their happiness was assured. They just had to wait a little longer, before getting it! But his wasn't! It wasn't even off the ground yet, and he was worried that if things didn't go the way his son's girlfriend's mother wanted them to…it wouldn't get off the ground!

He didn't expect anything spontaneous to happen. Both of the young couple had honored their no sex pledge, at least Katie thought her daughter had, and he was pretty sure Robert had too.

But since Katie had said what she said about it, he didn't want to risk facing the other side of her ultimatum.

So as he lay there comfortably in his own bed, about to fall asleep, feeling secure that the young couple was in their separate rooms fast asleep in their own beds, and his future with Katie was about to get off the ground. His eyes became heavy from lack of sleep, and just as he was about to close them. An alarming sound outside his room, like someone talking broke the silent, and caused his heart to start pounding. He sat up in bed wide awake, his heart beating so loud that he barely heard the two soft whispering voices coming from the other end of the hallway.

He got out of bed, walked to the door, and stepped out into the hall, hoping the voices he just heard were part of a bad dream he was having. But standing there in his robe, in the middle of the hallway, just past midnight, hearing voices, he knew it wasn't just a dream!

"Use protection," the voice said." It wasn't loud and clear, the sound was quick and low, like someone giving a command. It was a young female voice, and it came from the guest room.

There was a pause, he heard some moving around inside, than a man's voice said. "I can't, I don't have any," it was a slow pleading voice, almost like a begging sound. It didn't sound like Robert, he couldn't really tell though, it was sluggish and it sounded like the speaker was almost out of breath when he said it. But then, he thought to himself, who else could it be?

"I want to have your baby; he heard the female voice say, I really do."

There was another pause, and then a man's voice said. "Aren't you taking he pill?"

"No," he heard the female say. We both agreed not to have sex, till after we were married.

"I know the man said, but now is such a right time, and we will be married soon."

"I want to please you," the woman said. "You know I do, but I don't want to get pregnant."

"And you won't," the man answered!

"How can you be so sure," she asked?

"Before I have an ejaculation," he heard the man say.

Matt wanted to leave, he'd heard enough. He didn't want to hear any more. His heart was still pounding, and he felt betrayed.

He wanted to get back to his room. He turned to start back, but before he'd made his first step. He heard the man's voice again.

"I will take it out!" it said.

Matt covered his ears.He couldn't believe it. His son and his future daughter-in-law, engaging is such an act. In his own house, right under his nose. After he had clearly let it be known that he didn't want them to. He couldn't break it up now though, he thought, even if Katie wanted him to. He couldn't burst the door open, and tell them to stop. No, he said to himself, it wasn't that they were doing anything terribly wrong, after all they were young and in love. He just thought the two of them respected him more, than to let it happen here tonight. But they didn't, he murmured to himself as he walked slowly back towards his room. He lifted his head and looked across the hall. The door to Robert's room was open, and he walked towards it. The night light was on, and Matt looked in, and saw Robert's bed. It was empty! He turned and walked back to his own room and fell across the bed.

CHAPTER 20

Even though he had got up early the next morning, Robert and Kim had got up earlier. The young couple after sleeping soundly through the night couldn't wait for morning to come. So they could get out of bed, and talk to each other, and be together, after a long night of separation. Kim was especially anxious to find out if the wet dirt road outside had dried up enough for Robert to drive on and take her back home. Robert just wanted to get outside, and check on everything, and go for his usual walk.

Matt woke up from a nightmare dream, feeling tired and frightened. Wishing he could forget this one, and close his eyes and go back to sleep. But unlike the dreams he'd had before this one wouldn't go away. It was terrifying and filled with threats. Only near the end, was there a small indication that the girl would forgive him, and his attempts at winning her trust again, wasn't a complete failure after failing to convince her in the dream to let him see her again. He lay in bed, wide awake telling himself, there was no way she could have known what happened last night, unless she happened to guess right, or somehow just by looking, a mother could tell about such things. And yet in his dream, she

141

knew, and she blamed him for letting it happen! He knew it was just a dream, and he knew it wasn't real, but what happened in the dream was real. So real that he was afraid to close his eyes, afraid it would happen all over again.

In the dream he had taken Kim home, and Katie met them at the door, took one look at Kim, and told her to go inside the house. Then looked back at him, and said she knew her daughter was no longer a virgin. She accused him of letting his son take her daughter to bed after she had told him not to, and she reminded him of the warning she had given him earlier. That in doing so he would forfeit any chance he might have had to take her to bed.

He told her he tried to keep them apart; he even made sure they went to their separate rooms, before he went to bed himself. But no matter what he did, they were in love, and found a way to be together. She told him she didn't want to see him any more, but she did recognized a good man, and after he found her lottery ticket and gave it back to her. She knew she had seen one, and Kim had told her she liked the way he fixed her hair. So if he wanted to come and eat dinner with her sometimes, she reckoned it would be alright.

At least she didn't finalize their liaison Matt thought, after the dream had ended, and he lay in bed wide awake, trying to figure out if Katie could really tell just by looking at her daughter if she was still a virgin or not. Of course Matt told himself, if Kim did become pregnant later on after he'd brought her home. Katie would still say it happened at his place, and would still blame him for letting them sleep together. But by then, maybe she wouldn't consider what happened such a bad thing. Maybe she would even be glad of it, and because it happened at his place, might even start calling him Grandpa. But now he couldn't wait for daybreak, so he could get up and get some breakfast, and make himself a cup of that tasteless instant coffee. He turned over, and closed his eyes, and went back to sleep

Robert dried himself off from the shower, put some clean clothes on, then walked out to the kitchen where Kim was waiting, and sat down at the table. "How was your shower," she asked, as she watched him pull a chair out and sit down. "I hope I didn't use up all the hot water, taking mine."

"You didn't," he said. "But we could have saved a ton of it, if we'd taken one together."

"Maybe so she said smiling, but don't forget we're not alone, your father is still sleeping." She walked over to where he was sitting, and kissed him, then sat down in his lap. "I'm making a fresh pot of coffee, and when he gets up, I think it would be nice if we drank a cup with him. We can pretend we like it!"

"I can do that," he said wrapping his arms around her. "You smell so good, and you look even better. I can't wait till we're married," he said, pulling her close to him and kissing her on the neck. Let's go to your room," he whispered in her ear, moving his lips down her neck, and standing up. "Dad will sleep another hour, if we don't wake him up, and he won't hear a thing from your room."

"No she said, we can't here, not now, and put me back down. I don't want you to see the bed I sleep in, until we both can sleep in it together."

He sat back down in the chair, and pulled her close to him.

She found his mouth with her lips, and her kiss told him she couldn't wait either. The coffee in the percolator began perking and the sound startled her. She pulled away, jumped out of his lap, and stood standing near the stove, just as Matt walked into the kitchen.

"Good morning, he said, how are my son and his future bride doing? I hope both of you got up out of bed this morning, filled with energy, and looking forward to a great day."

"I know I am," he finished the sentence, looking at them both and smiling. He walked over and sat down across the table from Robert, then glanced over at the stove where Kim was standing. "I can't think of a better way to get it started, than sitting down to a fresh cup of hot percolated coffee. Especially when your son, and your future daughter-in-law are sitting there sharing it with you." He reached out and touched Robert on the arm. "Correction," he said, pausing then looking around the room. "There is one way that might be better, and that is... When you wake up in the morning to the smell of the rich aroma and hear the sound of the coffee perking, and you know she's making it just for you. Then she sits down at the table and drinks a cup with you, and you realize she doesn't even like it. But she wants to please you, so she's drinking it anyway."

Kim walks to the table, takes a napkin from the box and wipes the tear from her eye, then bends down and kisses him on the forehead. "Oh Matt, it's my pleasure to drink a cup of coffee with my future father-in-law. Robert and I both agree that there isn't a better way to start the day, than to meet at the table as a family and share together the things you like the most. It could only be better if mother was here to share it with us." She walked back to the stove, got three china cups from the cabinet, poured two cups of hot coffee, and brought them to the table, and placed them in front of the two men. Then walked back to the pot, poured her a cup, walked back, and sat down at the table and started drinking coffee with Matt and Robert.

"Well," Matt said, looking up at Kim as she poured him a second cup, then put the pot back on the stove and walked to the other side of the table and sat down beside Robert. "How did you find your new sleeping quarters? I trust it didn't take you too long to become accustomed to that bed. Its new, you're the first one to sleep on it. I guess you can say, you broke it in," he said looking at Robert, and laughing then winking at her. "I hope that mattress wasn't too hard."

"I hope it wasn't either," Robert spoke up and said, looking at her and smiling, then reaching out and grabbing her hand.

"Did you get enough sleep last night?"

"I did," he continued without giving her a chance to answer.

'I woke up only one time during the whole night. Turned my night light on, got up and went to the kitchen, and got a drink of water. Came right back, got in bed, and went right back to sleep."

"I got plenty of sleep, slept like a baby," Kim said looking at Robert and squeezing his hand, then letting it go, and looking at Matt. "That mattress was just right, not too hard, and not too soft. Put me right to sleep, although, I did watch a little TV first." She looked at Robert, then turned and looked again at Matt. "I do hope you will forgive me, though."

"For what," they both shouted out at the same time?

"I'm embarrassed to tell you," she said, looking at them both. "I feel like a little girl fixing to get a scolding from her mother for getting her dress dirty before church time. But I did do something wrong, so I guess I'd better tell you about it."

They looked at each other, then turned and looked at her.

"Well I'm not your mother, so I' m not going to scold you." Matt said, and "we're not getting ready to go to church, so you don't have to worry about getting your clothes dirty. And you need not fret about your mother finding out, I won't tell her either."

"So please tell us, what in heaven's name, have you done that was so terrible! It made you feel uncomfortable telling us about it!"

She folded her palms together, and brought them up in front of her face in a praying faction, and bowed her head. "I fell asleep watching a movie, and left the TV on," she said. "I turned it off this morning when I woke up. It stayed on all night long though, I am sorry. It's the first time I've ever done anything like that. I hope the noise didn't keep either one of you awake. I had it turned down low before I went to sleep, but with everyone in bed, and the noise level in the house down to zero. You probable thought I had the volume up too high, if you heard it."

"My dear girl," Matt said looking at Robert then back at her, and trying not to laugh. "That is nothing for you to be embarrassed about. I'm sure you're not the only one who has ever fallen asleep, while lying in bed watching a movie and awoke the next morning to the cheers of the Today's Show flashing bright light in your not yet fully awake eyes. In fact it happens all the time. I expect a good majority of those that it happens to, unlike you; don't feel that they've done anything wrong. But rather are embarrassed and somewhat angry at themselves, for not knowing how the movie ended. So don't say another word about it, pretty little lady. You certainly didn't do anything wrong. Robert and I both are just happy that you slept through it all."

Robert got up, and put his arms around Kim, and kissed her on the cheek. "I'm glad you fell asleep baby there are some porno films on after midnight, the kind that you're not old enough to watch."

"Oh yah she said, and you are! How come you know so much about it, you been watching them?

"No" he said, kissing her again, and then going back to his chair. "I got a friend at school, who told me about them. He said his cousin told him they were on after midnight on certain channels during the week.

"Well if they were on last night I didn't see them, I was asleep, and I hope you was too."

"I was sweetheart he said looking at her, and sitting back down, and don't you worry, I haven't seen any of them, and I don't want to either."

Matt pulled his chair out from the table. "Well he said, looking straight at Kim, I have heard that that they are on late at night in some cities. But really some of the movies you see on TV these days are just as shocking, and you don't have to wait till after midnight to see them. He got up, and pushed his chair back under his table. "Thanks for the coffee he said, you making it, made my day."

"I'm going to my room now, and call my office and tell them I'm not coming in today."

"I hope you like Raisin Brand Cereal for breakfast, Robert loves them, get him to fix you some. Oh, and if you still feel any guilt for leaving the TV on all night don't, your forgiven! You paid us back in full by breaking in that new mattress."

Matt called his office, and was told he was the only one that didn't come in for work this morning, and everyone there asked about him, and wished him a speedy recover. He thanked them and told them they were doing a great job, and reminded them to tell the customers he was alright, and would be back at work tomorrow. He sat down on the edge of the bed, and smiled to himself. Every time he called his staff, and told them he wasn't coming in for work that day, they always wished him a speedy recover, even thought he had a feeling they knew he wasn't sick. It was like they knew he was just taking the day off, and that was alright with them.

He was the boss, and he could goof off whenever he wanted to! It was a good thought though, to know that all his staff got along so great together. He thought the world of them, they were his family, and he told them so, every day. Without their friendly and professional attitude, the large number of repeat customer he enjoyed as well as the first timers. That came into his office, would undoubtedly have taken their business to another salon. He thanked his assistant again, and told her to tell everyone he missed seeing them too, then closed the phone. He leaned back and fell across the bed, and stared up at the ceiling. His salon wasn't the only one in town, and it wasn't the biggest, he thought. But he did think it was the busiest, and he truly believed it was the best.

He pulled himself up on the edge of the bed, and folded his hands together. "I wish I could believe as strongly, that those voices I head in the hallway last night came from a TV program, he said to himself. I want to believe that Kim accidentally did fall asleep while watching a movie, and left the TV on just like she said, and woke up this morning with it still playing. I'd like to think that when I looked into Robert's room and saw his empty bed. He really had just gotten up and gone to the kitchen to get a drink of water, and if I had checked a few minutes later, I would have found him back in his bed fast asleep. But I don't see how I could have heard someone speaking on a TV program, and so easily mistaken it for real live people talking in a near by room. But I was at the other end of the hallway, and the voices were soft and low, and I was what you might say half asleep, at the time, so I could have been mistaken. She could have fallen asleep and later during the night, an x rated movie came on, or a couple was about to make love on one of those sex shows that come on late at night, and that is what I heard. It's possible, I should give her the benefit of the doubt, she could be telling the truth. If she was, and one of those movies was on, I'm glad she was asleep, and didn't see it.

He got up and walked to the corner of the room, where his small desk was and picked up the piece of paper that had Katie's phone number written on it, then walked back to the bed.

Still he thought to himself, as he picked up the cell phone. I can't help but wonder if they made up the whole story, just to cover any noise they might have made in case I was awake and listening.

"Dad." Robert called out as he walked towards his father's room. "Kim and I are going outside for a little walk. I want to see if that road out there has dried up any, and I need to stretch my legs anyway," he said as he approached the room.

Matt opened the door, and looked out at Robert. "Ok he said, but don't stay out there too long. I want us both to take a look at that road together, before either one of us gets on it. But first before you take that walk, can you come inside for a minute, I want to tell you something."

"Sure Robert said, turning back around to face his dad, just let me tell Kim. Be right back honey, he called out, and then we'll go for that walk got to talk to dad now."

"Come in Robert, and close the door," Matt said. "I'll try to keep this short, because I know you want to get back to Kim. There's something I need to tell you, and then I want to ask you a question. Its none of my business, and I wouldn't bother you with it now. But I'm kind of in a tight spot, and I need your input on something. I haven't had a chance to tell you any of this before." He walked over to the closet, and pulled out a folded chair, opened it, and placed it beside his own, and told Robert to sit down. "It's been just you and me living in this old house all these years since your mother passed away. I've never been lonely, and I have you to thank for that. We've always been together, and it's been great, he said sitting down in a chair beside him. "But now you're getting married, and will be moving out with your new wife to another house, and I'll still be living here in this one." He got up and walked to the dresser, looked into the mirror, then walked back, and stood looking at Robert. "A man doesn't need to live alone, he needs companionship."

"What are you saying dad," Robert said looking up at him. "You want us to stay here in this house with you, after we're married?"

"No he said its right that you and your wife should move out." He sat back down in the chair, and turned and faced his son. "What I'm trying to tell you, is that I don't want to be lonely, and I'm worried that living in this old house all by myself, will make me that way. He lifted his shoulders and sat up straight in the chair, and looked at his son. "I'm not a lonely person Robert, but I am vulnerable to its influence, and already I'm beginning to feel lonely from just thinking about it" He got up and started walking back and forth across the floor. "No," he said, stopping and looking again at Robert. "You take your wife and get out of here, and make your own memories in your own house. Just like I made mine in this one, with you and your mother. But that's not what I asked you in here for," he said stopping, and sitting back down in the chair. "Yesterday he began, when I stopped off at the Convenient Store, before coming home like I usually do, I met a woman there. Who unknowing to me at the time was the woman that had caused me such road rage earlier, that I became so annoyed and ticked off, that I almost came completely unglued.

Ten minutes later, I held the door open for that same woman to come inside the store, and before I could recover myself. She walked right passed me, looked into my eyes, and without saying a single word stole my heart away with one simple smile." He put his hand over his mouth, and cleared his throat. "Son, the glow from that smile, lit me up like a Christmas Tree. I was in such a hurry to follow that woman. That I pulled that door closed behind me, rushed into the store, and literally pushed and shoved my way through the crowd till I stood directly behind her, in a line waiting to buy lottery tickets. You know how I dislike waiting in line for anything," he said, getting up and stretching his arms out in front of Robert. "Well son," he said dropping his arms and his voice to an almost whisper. "This was one time I didn't mind waiting at all. That woman smelled so good, I think I could have stood there the rest of the day!

He sat back down, and crossed his legs. "I'll try to hurry along, because I know you want to get back to Kim and go for that walk. I don't know what it was that brought all the people out. It must have been the slow rain, together with the lottery jackpot being higher than it had been in years. But I'm telling you that place was so crowded. That I believe all the people from town must have come to this one place to buy their tickets, and I think most of them were standing in front of me! Finely after what seemed like hours of standing in line, we reached the front, and she bought four lottery tickets, then stepped out, and began to walk away. I tried to keep my eyes on her while I was buying mine, but there was so many people there, that I soon lost site of her. At that instant, when she disappeared out of my site, I thought my heart would drop right out of my chest. I was so afraid she would disappear into the crowd, or leave the store, and I would never see her again. That I almost got out of line, and took off after her. If that clerk hadn't handed me my tickets at that very moment I'm afraid I would have! After I got my tickets, I got out of line, and started walking around the store, looking for her. I spotted her near the restaurant leaning against a chair, going through her purse. I didn't know what she was looking for, but as she closed it, a piece of paper fell out. She obvious didn't see it fall, because she closed her purse, and walked away. I walked over and hurriedly picked the paper up, noticed that it was a lottery ticket, and put it inside my shirt pocket. I saw it fall from her purse, so I knew it belonged to her, and I knew I had to find her and give it back. But now, as I followed her with my eyes, my heart began beating faster and the confidence inside me rose to an all time high. I had an excuse to talk to her now. I had something that was hers, and if she wanted to get it back, she would have to talk to me too!

Matt uncrossed his legs, started to stand up, changed his mind, and sat back down. "I caught up with her and just in time too," he said, looking at Robert. "She was reaching for the door knob, fixing to leave the building, when I called out. Don't leave Miss."

She stopped turned, and looked at me like I had just committed a crime. "Excuse me!" She said.

I started walking in her direction then stopped, and looked right at her, and said. "I have something that belongs to you!" That got her attention.

She looked around to see if help could be provided from the bystanders, should she need it then she looked back at me like I was a mad man. "What did you say," she almost shouted, a slight hint of cursorily beginning to show on her face.

"You dropped something from your purse, I found it, and now I just want to give it back to you," I said. "Well to make a long story short, I approached her, she didn't call for help, and she didn't leave the building." We talked, and I gave her back the lottery ticket. She thanked me, and marked a big X on it, and told me if it won, a large share would go to me. Then I offered to buy her a cup of coffee, she accepted, and we sat down at a booth for almost an hour and talked, and then we kissed.

"You kissed her right after you just met her!" Robert said, jumping to his feet and waving his arms in his father's face. "Didn't you think that might be just a little too soon? Wasn't you afraid she would slap your face, or maybe just get up and leave, he asked looking a little bewildered? He sat back down, and turned a gloomy, morbid look towards his dad. "Or was she just thanking you for giving her back the lottery ticket?"

Matt looked at Robert, and smiled. "Oh it was no thank you gesture son, and it was no accident either. She didn't just kiss me, we kissed each other. I'll admit, we both got caught up in the excitement of the moment." He paused briefly, and lowered his voice. "The moment when she discovered she had just kissed her daughter' boy friend's father, and got so exited about it. That she invited him to dinner the next day at her house. You can imagine how quick I was to accept such an offer, and then finding myself sitting at the table in a romantic situation with my future daughter-in-law's mother. My cup truly had run over, I was on cloud nine!" He paused again, glanced at Robert, saw the almost shocked, yet surprised look on his face, waited a moment then continued. "Well son, he said leaning forward in his chair, now you know why I was late getting home yesterday. I was in town at a restaurant getting acquainted with your future mother-in-law."

CHAPTER 21

Robert sat there for the next minute, without moving, just looking at his dad. "I can't believe it," he finally said, getting up from his chair. "You met Kim's mother, and you two got acquainted, and now she's fixing dinner for you at her house."

"That's right Matt said letting out a little chuckle, got to keep this dating thing all in the family."

"When dad?" Robert said, "When are you going to her house?"

"Tonight," Matt answered. "Right after you take Kim home, if I can get myself together, and that road out there dries up enough."

"That's great, Robert said, we can all have dinner together tonight. I'm glad for you, I'm glad for both of you. Kim will be tickle pink when I tell her."

"Of course you and Kim will be there hours before me, Matt said, cutting Robert off. "I haven't been out on a date in so long, it will probably take me all those hours to get myself ready."

Robert pulled his chair a little closer to Matt. "I guess I can tell you now," he said, leaning over and smiling at his dad. Both of you were supposed to meet tomorrow night on a blind date anyway! Kim and I were going out for dinner that night, and she was going to bring her mother along, and I was going to bring you. I was going to ask you about it tomorrow."

Matt patted Robert on the shoulder and laughed. "Thanks son he said, I know we both would have enjoyed meeting each other. But you do remember I told you I also had a question I wanted to ask you? Well now I must ask you that question, and your answer could determine whether we keep this dating thing in the family or not." He walked over to the bed, sat down on the edge, then got back up and went back to his chair beside Robert and stood beside it. "Earlier today," he began putting his hand over his mouth, and clearing his throat. "When I talked to Kim's mother on the phone" he said. "She reminded me of what she had told me earlier after she found out that I was your father, and Kim was staying overnight with you in my house." He folded his palms together, cracked his knuckles, and sat down. "She said both of them had talked a few times before about this, and her daughter told her just last week. That she felt Robert was the right man, and it hurt her to keep refusing him. But long ago before he died, when she was a little girl, she made a promise to her sick father. That before any man knew her, she would be married to him first!" Matt crossed his legs, uncrossed them, then got up, and began pacing the floor. He stopped and stood for a moment in front of his son.

"This all came about," she told me, he continued, as he sat back down in the chair.

"When at a young age her father began reading the Bible to her, each night before she went to bed. After he had read Genesis 4&1, she stopped him, and asked what that part about Adam knew his wife Eve meant. In his most tender fatherly way she said, he did his best to tell her in his own words what it meant. There

155

was only one man back then in God's new world. It was the beginning of everything, he started out telling her, and his name was Adam. And God wanted a companion for Adam, so he wouldn't be alone, so he met a woman, and her name was Eve. Then God made a little thing called feelings, and he brought them together, and gave it to them, and they liked it, and God saw that it was good. But God said I need something else, something that will make them want to come together, and stay together as one. So he created another feeling, and told them they could enjoy this new feeling anytime. But it was his wish, that before they did, they make a commitment to each other to stay together, and use this feeling only among themselves. And he brought them together, and gave it to them, and he called this new feeling marriage. And God married them, and told them they were as one now, and they could come together and make more people for his new world. And he gave them yet another feeling, and it made them want to come together and make special people like themselves, and he called them children. And he called this new feeling, family. And he saw that it was good, and God, put all his new feelings together, and called it love, and said I will leave it here with my people in my new world.

"He could do that," her father told her, stopping his explaining, because they were his people, he created them, and they were living in his world."

Kim was very inquisitive at that age, and she asked her father if Eve didn't want to marry Adam, would she still have to, before they could come together, and make more people? He told her that God had made Eve so she could become Adam's wife, and Eve indeed wanted to marry Adam and come together as one, and make more people. She was far to young to know what coming together, and making more people meant, and after a few more questions, that even he couldn't answer. He just gave up and told her that in those days, when the Bible said that Adam knew Eve his wife. It meant that they came together, and he made love to her! Of course she didn't know what that meant either. So he just came right out and told her that coming together, meant making love, and making more people, meant having more babies. It is still God's wish he said, that people come together and have babies, but only if they are married and want more babies. And if she didn't understand what all that meant, she would just have to wait till she was a little older, because he didn't know anything else to tell her! She may not have understood all of what her father did tell her, she said. But I think she understood what the word "Knew" meant." Because that's when she made the promise!

Matt got up and began pacing the floor again, then stopped and stood in front of Robert.

"Moving right on," he said as he looked at his son and smiled, then sat back down beside him.

"What she said next, I believe, came right from her heart, and it was directed straight at me. What I want to drive home to you right now is, and these are her exact words. When my daughter left her house, going to your house. She had never been with a man before, and when your son leaves his house, bringing my daughter back to her house. If I had any intent of ever seeing her again, I'd see to it that she returned, never having been with a man! I don't know what she expected me to do," Matt said, "telling you sooner might have helped, I don't know. But I do know that I want to see her again, and if that road out there dried up any at all I would have every intention of telling her that today!

"Good for you Dad, Robert said, leaning forward in his chair, and don't sweat it, we both believe as you do, and we have ever intendances of seeing her today too."

Matt stood up and walked to the other side of the room, then came back and sat down. "Thanks Robert, he said looking at him and smiling, I knew I could count on you. You know son, Kim's mother wanted me to tell you this, and I'm not just saying it. I think maybe it might have been what she expected me to do. She also wanted me to tell you, that she likes you, and she thinks you're a good man. I told her that I knew you was a good man!" Matt got up, and walked towards the door. "Now son," he said, standing by the door, and looking back at Robert.

"You better go get Kim, and go for that walk."

"What about that question you wanted to ask me," Robert said?

"Oh it wasn't important, Matt said, besides, I think you knew what it was anyway!"

CHAPTER 22

Katie looked at Papa, from across the table. She had just finished eating her lunch, and was on her second cup of coffee. Papa had a slice of ham between two pieces of toast, and was sipping on his first cup of cranberry juice. Todd had just eaten his club sandwich, and was about to leave the table, when Katie told him to sit back down, she had something to tell them both. "You remember," she started out saying, looking back and forth at each of them, her voice a little low, like she was still searching for the right words. I told you that I nearly had an accident in the parking lot, before going into the store to buy lottery tickets, and that I met a man inside the store, who said he was Robert's father."

"Yes, they both answered at the same time."

"Well she said, that man just called me, and sure enough he is Robert's father, and I think he was also the man who caused me to almost have an accident. Kim's with them now, and their bringing her home tonight, and I asked them both to stay and have dinner with us. Remember I told you earlier that another guest might be coming with Robert? Well I'm pretty sure that other guest was the driver involved in the same mishap I was involved in, but he doesn't know I was involved in it." She took a big swallow of her coffee, set the cup down on the table leaned over, looked at both of them, and smiled. "I don't want either one of you mentioning anything about the accident. Is that clear," she said! I will tell him myself later when the time is right, and we both understand it a little more. That little mishap, played a large part in bringing us together, but right now, I suspect he feels like he'd like to beat that other driver's head in. So I don't want to scare him away by letting him find out too soon, that I was that other driver!"

"I also mention to you Papa, that I had lost one of my lottery tickets, and was about to leave the store, without realizing I'd lost it, when a man, a total stranger I might add, stopped me, and told me he'd found it. Well Papa, she said rising up in her seat, and looking at him, that was your ticket! She sat back down, but continued looking at him. "He gave it back, but I promised him half of it, if it won." She swallowed the last of her coffee, and then sat the cup back down on the table. "That stranger that kept me from making a fool of myself when I was about to accuse the cashier of keeping one of my tickets was the same stranger that stood behind me for almost an hour yesterday in the Convention Store, waiting in line to buy his lottery tickets as soon as I finished buying mine."

She picked up the coffee cup, looked at it, seen that it was empty, and sat it back down on the table. "After we both got our tickets, I started walking towards the door, on my way out when he approached me, and offered to buy me a cup of coffee. Well let me tell you, I was shocked and pleased at the same time. I quickly asked myself what his motive could be. I wasn't well dressed, my hair looked a mess, and I barely had any makeup on. Yet there he was, looking at me!" My mind quickly flashed a caution sign. I stopped, turned around and looked back at him. He did look familiar, like I'd seen him before, but I couldn't place him, and I certainly was in no mood to talk to a stranger. Yet it was satisfying. I haven't had an offer of that type from a man in so long that I'd forgotten there was still such a thing." She paused and looked back at them both, then continued. "Of course I haven't made myself available to them either," she said smiling.

"You are a very attractive young woman," Papa said, standing up and looking at her with a half smile on his face. "I have wondered from time to time, why you never dated?"

"My Mama's been waiting for that right man to come along," Todd said, looking up at his mother and smiling.

"Thank you Papa, and thank you son. I think maybe through some divine purpose that I don't fully understand yet; that right man has finally came along. Well like I was saying, she continued, holding her head down, like she was still thinking of that diving purpose. I didn't want to spend any more of my time talking to a stranger. I just wanted to walk out of there, and get in my car, and drive home and start cooking dinner. So my first thoughts were to ignore him, and keep on walking. Then I remembered he held the door open for me when I first came into the store. So wanting to repay an act of kindness I let him buy me a cup of coffee!" Well that first cup, led to another cup, and after a while of inductions and talking about ourselves. I started telling him about my daughter, and he started telling me about his son, and before long it became obvious to us, that our two children were dating each other! Of course that was news we both enjoyed hearing, since we were on the verge of starting a romantic advance ourselves. And even if we'd known it then, we probably would not have admitted it. But the thought of having a double wedding, and keeping all the participating members in one family was such a delightful thought, even if it was buried in the back of our subconscious mind!"

Katie got up from the table; brought some more juice for Papa, told him it was for saying she was still a young woman. Kissed Todd lightly on the check, and said that he was such a sweet kid, fixed herself another cup of coffee, and sat back down at the table. "I'm telling you this she said, picking up her cup, and looking at both of them because there's been a change of plans. Robert's father is coming with him, and instead of having dinner, here at my place, we're all going out for a pizza buffet. It was his idea, most everyone young and old loves a good hot pizza he said, and what better way to get acquainted and put everyone at ease, than to sit around the table eating and enjoying one of American's most favorite meals. "I know that's ok with you, Todd," she said, watching him jump up and yell "all right! But I wanted to make sure it was ok with Papa too."

"You like pizza don't you Papa," Todd said, jumping up and down again, and pulling at his arm.

"Tell Mama its ok."

"Its ok Papa said looking at Katie and smiling. I love pizza!"

"After we've all eaten, Kim and Robert are going for a ride, I think" she continued. They want to be alone together, so they can talk. After all they are getting married!" She patted Todd on the top of his head. "And then you and me and Papa and our guest are going back to my place. Later on as the night approaches, you and Papa are going to bed and me and my guest will be alone, and then we can talk." She swallowed the rest of her coffee, stood up and moved close to each of them. "Tomorrow when Robert and his father comes back for a visit if you two can act like a normal family, and don't embarrass me too much, we can all talk again, and then later maybe even go for a ride together.